3 NINJAS
KICK BACK

A novelization by Todd Strasser
from a screenplay by Mark Saltzman
based on a screenplay by Simon Sheen

SCHOLASTIC INC.
New York Toronto London Auckland Sydney

TRISTAR PICTURES PRESENTS A SHEEN PRODUCTION IN ASSOCIATION WITH BEN-AMI/LEEDS PRODUCTIONS A CHARLES T. KANGANIS FILM "3 NINJAS KICK BACK" VICTOR WONG
MAX ELLIOTT SLADE SEAN FOX EVAN BONIFANT AND SAB SHIMONO MUSIC RICHARD MARVIN EXECUTIVE SIMON SHEEN YORAM BEN-AMI PRODUCER SIMON SHEEN
SCREENPLAY MARK SALTZMAN PRODUCED JAMES KANG MARTHA CHANG ARTHUR LEEDS DIRECTED CHARLES T. KANGANIS

Cover photo by Ron Slenzak.
Interior photos supplied by Youshiharu Nushida and Yoshiyaki Shina.

If you purchased this book without a cover, you should be aware that this book is stolen property. It was reported as "unsold and destroyed" to the publisher, and neither the author nor the publisher has received any payment for this "stripped book."

ISBN 0-590-48450-8

12 11 10 9 8 7 6 5 4 3 2 1   4 5 6 7 8 9/9

Printed in the U.S.A.   01

First Scholastic printing, May 1994

To the two ninjas of Manor Lane,
Jake and Caleb Shapiro

Chapter 1

Rocky Douglas, age fourteen, grabbed a branch and pulled himself a little farther up the tree. His green ninja mask shifted slightly on his face and he straightened it. One more branch and he would reach the hemp climbing rope that hung from above. He grabbed it with one hand and straightened his ninja outfit, retying the green belt and knotting it more firmly around his waist. Trouble was coming and he had to be prepared.

Rocky took a deep breath and let it out slowly. It was time to hide and wait. The early morning summer sun sparkled through the thick green leaves of the trees around him, and the air was dry and warm. He squeezed the rope in his hands and looked down at the dusty dirt trail winding through the woods and past the tree where he hid. Be patient, he told himself. The evil ninja will come. Rocky was the patient one, unlike his brother Colt, who had a quick temper and even quicker hands. Rocky was strong, solid, and cool. His real name was Samuel, but his grandfather, Mori Shintaro, said he was like a rock, and so he had taken the ninja name of Rocky.

Snap . . . The sound of a breaking twig pierced the silence. Instantly alert, Rocky looked down through the branches. He caught a glimpse of someone dressed in black and wearing a painted black-and-red mask. Yes, just as he had expected, the evil ninja was coming.

Again Rocky squeezed the rope in his hands and pulled it taut. The evil ninja was jogging down the trail, clearly not expecting an attack this deep in the woods.

Rocky knew he had to time it perfectly. At just the precise moment he gripped the rope tight and launched himself out into the air. Down he swung, feet out, ready to smash the evil ninja to the ground. But at the very last second, the evil ninja suddenly looked up.

"*Yah!*" With a grunt, he jumped out of Rocky's path and rolled into the underbrush beside the trail.

Rocky quickly let go of the rope and landed on the ground near the ninja. He instantly assumed battle stance and attacked with a vicious series of kicks and blows.

"*Cha! Ooof! Uh! Yah!*"

The black ninja met each kick and blow with an expertly executed block. Rocky wasn't surprised by the ninja's skill. He was actually setting the evil one up for something that *would* surprise him.

Just when he hoped the ninja would least expect it, Rocky lunged forward, throwing his whole body into the air.

But the evil ninja saw the move coming and deftly ducked under Rocky's swinging arms and legs.

Thud! Rocky slid into the middle of the dirt trail, kicking up a cloud of dust. He immediately hopped to his feet and assumed a defensive stance, certain a surprise attack would come through the dust.

But nothing happened.

As the dust settled, Rocky looked around, puzzled. The evil ninja was gone.

Wearing his blue ninja mask and outfit, Colt Douglas, age twelve, crouched on a tree limb high above a mountain stream. Below him an old tree trunk spanned the bubbling stream like a bridge. It was the only way across, and Colt knew it was the perfect place to trap the evil ninja.

Colt balanced on the branch with his *bo*, a long, wooden fighting stick. The *bo* stick was old and worn smooth from many hours of practice. But this was more than practice.

Colt's heart beat fast. Where was the black ninja? He should have come by now. Colt knew he shouldn't be so impatient, but he couldn't help it. It was part of his nature, and one of the reasons his grandfather said he had the spirit of a young and wild horse. Colt preferred his nickname to his real name, which was Jeffrey.

Crack! Colt heard the sound and looked up. On the other side of the stream the

4

black ninja had broken off a branch of a sapling to use for balance while crossing the tree-trunk bridge. Now he started inching his way across the log over the stream.

Above him, Colt felt every muscle in his body tense. The element of surprise was on his side, and he wanted to time it perfectly.

The black ninja reached the middle of the tree trunk. Colt stepped off the branch above. *Thunk!* He landed on the log right in front of the enemy.

"*Yow!*" Gripping the *bo* stick like a baseball bat, Colt swung as hard as he could.

"*Tah!*" Somehow the ninja managed to duck. He quickly swung his own stick low, trying to knock Colt's feet out from under him. Colt jumped in the air and did a backflip, but his feet came down on the rounded edge of the tree trunk and he slipped.

"*Whoops!*" As he fell off, he managed to grab a broken stump sticking out from the log.

For a moment Colt hung by one hand over the rippling stream. When he pulled himself back up, the evil ninja had disappeared.

*   *   *

Colt and Rocky's little brother, Tum Tum, age ten, crouched behind a bush by the side of the wooded trail. He wore a yellow ninja mask and his yellow ninja outfit. A long strand of red licorice hung from the mouth of the mask, and he slowly chewed on it, savoring its delicious cherry flavor.

Tum Tum's real name was Michael, but his grandfather said that his energy and spirit came from his tummy, and this was the origin of his ninja name.

Suddenly Tum Tum sensed someone coming down the trail toward him. He peeked through the bush and saw the black ninja moving cautiously, ever alert.

At just the right moment, Tum Tum leaped out from the bush and attacked, just missing the black ninja, who did a backflip and landed several yards away.

"Hold him!" Tum Tum heard Rocky shout. Looking down the trail behind the ninja, Tum Tum saw his brothers running toward him. Colt had his *bo* stick, and Rocky was carrying his *bo* stick and two tree branches.

The black ninja saw them coming, too,

and quickly picked up a heavy stick of his own.

"Here!" Rocky tossed one of the branches to Tum Tum, and the three brothers surrounded the black ninja.

"*E-yah!*" They all attacked at once. The black ninja jumped and spun, blocking their sticks with his. His skill was awesome, but pitted against three equally skilled opponents, he couldn't defend himself for long.

Each brother fought in his own style. Colt swung his *bo* stick wildly, showing his athletic prowess. Tum Tum fought fearlessly, showing his spirit. Rocky fought craftily, looking for opportunities to surprise and confuse the evil one.

It was Rocky who finally knocked the stick out of the black ninja's hands.

Now the evil ninja was defenseless and surrounded by the three boys. Hands out and feet spread, he spun around looking for an escape route, but the brothers made sure there was none.

Colt and Tum Tum watched Rocky for the sign, for he was the oldest and acted as their leader. Rocky nodded.

"*Charge!*" The three brothers shouted and closed in with swinging sticks.

Pop! Poof!

They heard a small explosion, and the air was suddenly filled with smoke. Unable to see, the boys charged onward, swinging their sticks.

Crack! Snap! Whack!

The sticks slammed into each other.

"Hold it!" Rocky shouted.

The boys stopped fighting. A slight breeze blew the smoke away, and they realized the black ninja was gone.

Tum Tum angrily pulled off his mask. "Why'd you get in my way, Colt? I had him."

"You didn't get near him, Tum Tum," Colt replied, pulling off his own mask and pushing his dirty-blond hair out of his eyes.

"Did too, didn't I, Rocky?" Tum Tum turned to his oldest brother.

Rocky took off his mask, ran his fingers through his brown hair, and sighed. "Looks like Grandpa wins again."

"So where is he?" Colt asked, leaning on his *bo* stick and looking around.

"Where do you think?" Rocky pointed upward.

The boys looked up into a nearby tree. Standing on a branch ten feet above them was the black ninja. He took off his mask and smiled down at them. It was their grandpa Mori, of course.

"How'd you do that, Grandpa?"

"Ah, there are some secrets I can never tell." Grandpa Mori jumped off the branch and landed softly on the trail beside them. "Come, boys, sit down."

They sat at the base of the tree and watched as their grandfather took out a bag of peas and a box of raw spaghetti from his black ninja suit. Their grandfather was a short, stocky man with thinning hair, a friendly face, and a wispy white beard.

"Lunch already?" Tum Tum asked, licking his lips.

"*Raw* spaghetti?" Colt wrinkled his nose. "Aren't you gonna cook it?"

"Hey, I like it crispy." Tum Tum took several strands out of the box and munched hungrily on them.

"You are totally weird," said Colt, shaking his head.

"This food is not for eating," Grandpa Mori told them. "It is for learning."

The boys watched as their grandfather held up one strand of spaghetti and a single pea. He carefully poked the spaghetti

9

through the center of the pea. Then he stood up and hung the spaghetti on a tree branch.

"Keep your eyes on the pea," Mori instructed them as he drew his knife out of his robes. "Wipe out all your thoughts and focus your energy on it. You will see the pea grow bigger right in front of your eyes."

"Yeah, right," Tum Tum muttered doubtfully.

"Shut up!" Colt hushed him.

"Just try it, Tum Tum," said Rocky.

Their grandfather was still staring at the pea. "When it gets as big as a bull's-eye . . ."

In a flash he whipped the knife around and sliced the little pea in half. He tossed the sliced pea to Colt.

"Oh, wow!" Colt gasped in amazement. "Right through the middle."

"Now we can have split pea soup!" Tum Tum cried.

Rocky and Colt groaned. Even Grandpa Mori had to shake his head in wonder. "Come, boys," he said. "Your training continues."

Chapter 2

Just as they had every summer before this one, the three brothers trained in the ninja arts with their grandfather. The boys liked being up in the woods, away from their suburban neighborhood and their parents. Although their grandfather's training was very rigorous and left them exhausted at night, they enjoyed it, and had learned a great deal.

Each day's training ended with a session on the "light up the eyes" dummy. This was a life-size human dummy Grandpa Mori had made. It had a gruesome face and two large red lightbulbs for eyes. When the dummy was hit in certain places, the eyes would light up.

The boys gathered around the dummy, but before they began their training session, their grandfather lectured them. It was a warm, peaceful evening. The sun was low and red in the sky, just minutes from setting. The dummy and the trees around them had a red tint from the setting sun.

"Relax, boys," Grandpa Mori advised. "Look within yourselves. Close your eyes. Take deep breaths."

The boys did as they were told.

"Now attack the dummy," Grandpa Mori said.

Each boy rose and faced the dummy.

"And remember," their grandfather said, "a ninja is body, and . . ."

"Heart!" Tum Tum cried, kicking hard and true.

The eye-lights flashed red.

"Mind!" Rocky shouted, hitting the dummy hard.

Again the eye-lights flashed.

"And spirit!" added Colt, running up and blasting the dummy so hard the eyes not only lit up, they popped right out of the dummy's head!

Grandpa Mori watched with a smile. "Boys, come, I have something to tell you."

The boys assembled in a line before him.

"Are you gonna tell us what's for dinner?" Tum Tum asked.

"You're not gonna tell us it's time to go home, are you?" Colt asked.

"Chill, guys," Rocky said. "Let Grandpa speak."

Grandpa Mori stood before them, looking solemn. "Boys, you have reached a crucial juncture in your training."

Tum Tum frowned. "What's that mean?"

"It means we've reached an important point," Rocky said.

"I have taught you all I know," their grandfather said. The boys started to smile proudly, but their grandfather was not finished. "It is now time for you to study with a teacher greater than myself."

The smiles quickly faded from the boys' faces. Grandpa Mori turned and started back toward his cabin.

"You mean, you don't want to teach us anymore?" Colt asked as the boys followed, giving each other concerned looks.

"I would teach you if I could, but I can't," their grandfather replied.

"But you're the only one who's ever taught us," Tum Tum whined. "I don't want to study with someone else."

"It is important for your training," Grandpa Mori explained. "You must never stop learning."

He opened the door to his cabin and held it for his sad-faced grandsons.

"I'm not doing it," Tum Tum said stubbornly, crossing his arms. "There's no one around here who knows more than you."

"You're right," said Grandpa Mori, following them inside. "There is no one around *here* who does."

"Well, that's just what I was say — " Tum Tum began.

"Wait a minute." Rocky cut his brother off and turned to his grandfather. "What did you mean, not around *here*?"

"I mean you must go somewhere else to study," Grandpa Mori said.

"Like where?" Tum Tum asked.

"Japan."

The boys' eyes went wide. *Japan?* That

was where it all began! Japan was where the best ninjas in the world lived! Japan was the ultimate for ninja arts!

"Japan!" Colt gasped in wonder. "We really get to go to Japan?"

"*Ya-hoo!*"

"*Awesome!*"

"*Incredible!*"

The boys began shouting and dancing and giving each other high-fives.

"Boys . . ." Grandpa Mori tried to calm them down. "Boys."

"*Can you believe it?*"

"*It's gonna be so cool!*"

"Quiet!" Grandpa Mori shouted.

The boys quieted down.

"I must go to Japan next week," Grandpa Mori said. "To my hometown of Konang. I have arranged for you to come with me, to study with the grand master."

"All right! The grand master!" Tum Tum jumped in the air and started throwing chops and kicks at invisible foes. "*E-yah!*"

Meanwhile, Grandpa Mori went over to the wall. He took down a picture, revealing a panel on the wall. Behind the panel was a secret compartment.

"Wow, I never knew that was there," Rocky said.

Grandpa Mori nodded. "That was the point."

The boys watched as their grandfather lifted a silver dagger from the secret compartment. Beautiful etchings covered the blade, and the handle was wrapped in gold-and-purple silk. The boys crowded in toward their grandfather, jostling each other.

"Cool!"

"Awesome!"

"Hey, let *me* see it!"

But Grandpa Mori held it away from them. "Stop! First I will tell you a story. Sit."

The boys quickly sat on the floor. Grandpa Mori sat down before them and crossed his legs.

"Fifty years ago, when I was just about your age, I fought for the honor of receiving this dagger," he said.

"Fought who?" Colt asked.

"I will tell you in a moment," Grandpa Mori replied.

"What's so interesting about this dagger?" Tum Tum asked.

"There was a legend about the dagger and a samurai sword," Grandpa Mori said. "According to the legend they could open the door to a cave of gold and other riches."

"You mean, like a key?" Tum Tum asked.

"Exactly," his grandfather said. "The old master who taught me my skills told me the whole story when the dagger was passed along."

"But who'd you fight for it?" Colt persisted.

"A young man named Koga," Grandpa Mori said. "He was very greedy, and even though I defeated him for the dagger, he tried to steal it from me."

"Wow, what happened?" Tum Tum asked.

"He tried to jump me with a *bo* stick but I held onto the dagger and accidentally cut him on the cheek."

"And then what happened?" Rocky asked.

"He ran off," Grandpa Mori said with a shrug. "We were just boys playing a long time ago. But now I must take the dagger back and present it to the winner of the ninja tournament, just as it was presented to me fifty years ago."

17

"What about the cave of gold, Grandpa?" Tum Tum asked. "Can we visit it when we go to Japan?"

"Weren't you listening?" Colt asked. "He said we'd need the sword to get in, twerp."

"Bigger twerp," Tum Tum shot back.

"*Biggest*," countered Colt.

Tum Tum jumped up and assumed battle position. In a flash, Colt faced him. Tum Tum was just about to spring into the air and strike when Grandpa Mori jumped between them.

"Boys, boys," he cautioned them. "I told you it is just a legend. Some people believe it, but I personally think there is no cave of gold."

"But what if there was?" Colt asked.

"You would still need the sword as well as the dagger to get in," his grandfather said.

"Well, where is the sword?" Tum Tum asked.

"No one knows," his grandfather replied.

Chapter 3

But someone did know. On the other side of the world, from the roof of a modern hillside building lit by a full moon, a man in black lowered a rope. Moments later the man crawled over the edge of the roof and began to rappel silently down the side. He reached the ground and looked up at the sign above the glass front doors. Large silver letters spelling Japan Museum of History reflected the moonlight.

The man in black looked around. The parking lot was empty, the road leading up the hill to it, dark. From under his robes the man drew out a small electronic device with several wires. He slid one wire into the slot in the door used for identification cards. Another wire went into the magnetic keyhole. The man in black turned a dial on the device until he heard the lock click. He quickly pulled open the door and stepped inside.

The building was very quiet and almost completely dark. As the man stepped silently through the lobby, a beam of moonlight caught his face, revealing that he was not young, and illuminating a long, distinctive scar on his cheek. The man passed through the light, and now it fell on a display case with a poster announcing the museum's current exhibit: *A Collection of Rare, Classic Samurai Swords.*

At the entrance to the exhibit room, the man stopped. Inside were glass cases holding magnificent swords. Some had beautifully etched solid-gold blades. Others had handles encrusted with jewels. The man in black merely glanced at these. He did not see what he was looking for, but he knew it was there.

He took a step toward the entrance to the room, then stopped suddenly, as if he'd just thought of something. From a small pouch in his robes he took out some white powder and blew it into the air. As the powder drifted through the entrance of the room, some of it began to sparkle with red light. Soon he could see three bars of red crossing the entrance of the exhibit hall. One was at knee height, the next at his waist, and the third parallel with his shoulders.

The man in black was confident there was no bar of light higher than that. Stepping back several yards from the exhibit entrance, he took a running jump and expertly sprang into a front flip, clearing the highest red-light bar with the ease of a ninja master.

Now he was inside the exhibit. With deliberate slowness he inspected each of the glass cases, passing up swords of enormous value. Finally he found what he was looking for in a small case toward the back of the exhibit. The sword inside the case appeared unexceptional, but for the man in black it was a prize worth impossible risk.

To be certain it was indeed the right sword, he pulled a penlight from his robe and kneeled down. He flicked on the light and illuminated the small plaque inside the case that read: *Ritual Samurai Sword from Konang*.

The man in black smiled to himself. From his robe he next took out a *shiruken* ninja star with a razor-sharp edge. With this he carefully cut a hole in the glass display case, and lifted out the prize.

Finally it was in his possession. He had waited fifty years for this moment.

Backtracking toward the lobby, he once again came to the entrance of the exhibit hall and blew the white powder. The three red bars of light appeared in the floating cloud of dust, and the man backed up and prepared to vault over them. He ran and jumped.

Brinnngggg! Even before his feet touched the polished tile floor, the alarm burst on. The man cursed to himself, knowing he'd somehow broken one of the bars of red light. There was no time to lose now; he had to get back to the roof.

He ran through an exit door and into a stairwell, suddenly coming face-to-face with two guards in green uniforms.

"Stop!" one shouted in Japanese, but the man in black vaulted over a metal banister and onto the stairs. The two guards raced around the banister and started up the stairs, but the man turned and expertly kicked.

Whomp! He hit the guards squarely in their chests and knocked them backward down the stairs.

The man in black raced up the stairs three steps at a time and came to the roof. There in the moonlight, he could see a guard with a gun, who was staring with a puzzled expression at a black batwing-shaped hang glider. The man in black stepped quickly and quietly up behind him, but the guard suddenly turned.

The man in black grabbed him, but the guard managed to pull the gun's trigger.

POW! A single shot echoed into the night. The man quickly disarmed the guard and knocked him out. There was no time to lose. Already the man in black could hear shouts and footsteps as more guards followed the sound of the shot. He hurried to the black hang glider and slid into the harness, strapping it tight. He reached into his robe to make sure he still had the sword, then stepped up on the edge of the roof and jumped.

Whoosh! In no time he was gliding quickly through the air away from the building, toward the distant lights of downtown Tokyo.

Bang! Bang! Bang! Glancing back over his shoulder, the man in black saw the flashes of light as the guards fired in vain at him. He knew he would be extremely difficult to hit, because he was a black figure against a black night sky.

It is as close as a man can come to being invisible, the man thought as he glided away through the night over buildings and houses that contained thousands of sleeping souls. It was as if he were a silent wraith flying onward toward the glowing center of Tokyo.

A little while later he saw a tall office building shimmering in the moonlight. The man in black shifted his weight and expertly maneuvered the batwing's cables to descend. Moments later he touched down in a parking lot behind the building. After releasing himself from the harness, he pulled the batwing into the shadows, then entered the building and took the elevator up.

The elevator opened on the highest floor, and the man in black hurried out, looking around him carefully. Not that he expected to run into anyone at that time of night, but he wasn't about to take any chances. He strode quickly down the hall and let himself into a large office decorated with black carpeting, dark walls, and black leather couches.

He carried the sword to a broad black desk and sat down. Flicking on a small reading light, he slowly withdrew the ancient sword from its sheath and gently caressed its blade. An evil smile creased his lips. Finally he had the first half of what he needed. Now all he had to do was get the second half.

The man in black put the sword down. A long red-white-and-blue envelope caught his eye. Excellent, he thought. It's come. He quickly reached for the envelope and tore it open. Two black-and-white photographs fell out onto the desk. The first was of the dagger Mori planned to bring to Japan. The second photo was of Mori himself. The man in black studied Mori's wizened old face and thinning gray hair.

So, he thought grimly, this is what has become of the boy who defeated me so many years ago. I've waited fifty years for my revenge. Little does he suspect that the battle is not over.

Chapter 4

Halfway across the world from Japan, Mori gathered his three grandsons together and spoke to them. They were standing on a grassy field. It was a pristine summer day. The sun was high and the sky was blue.

"Before you go to Japan, you must be tested on this field of battle," Mori said solemnly. "Remember what I have taught you. Concentration, restraint, control, and unity. We are four strands of a rope."

The boys placed their hands together.

"Separately, they snap," their grandfather continued. "Together, they are strong."

The boys grinned. Colt tipped his Dragons baseball cap down. All three boys were wearing their baseball outfits and carrying their blue ninja bags. Today was the final game of the baseball championships. Grandpa Mori had brought them home to play it.

"Hey, Mori!" someone shouted.

The boys and their grandfather turned and saw Sam Douglas, the boys' father, across the ballfield, waving at them from the green wooden dugout. He was the coach of the Dragons.

"Leave the ninja stuff for up at your cabin," Sam shouted. "Come on, guys, this is the big one! Hit it!"

Rocky turned to his brothers. "Time to warm up."

The boys joined the other members of the Dragons on the field. Colt got into his position as shortstop and started throwing the ball around to the other infielders. Rocky stepped onto the pitcher's mound and started throwing warm-up pitches to his father, who squatted with the catcher's mitt behind home plate.

Tum Tum had gone into the dugout to

pull on his catcher's gear. After he had it all on, he started to run out onto the field. Then something caught his eye — the hot dog vendor pushing his silver cart! With his shin guards and chest protector flapping, and his face mask riding on his head, Tum Tum quickly jogged over to the vendor. The wonderful smell of cooking hot dogs filled the air.

"Two, please," he said. "Make 'em on whole wheat buns."

Meanwhile, Sam Douglas squatted behind home plate, taking pitches from Rocky. His son looked a little nervous and tight. That was understandable, considering the importance of today's game. But Rocky's pitches were coming in right through the middle of the strike zone, just where the other team's batters wanted them.

"Keep it down, son," Sam reminded him.

Rocky nodded, wound up, and threw another pitch. It was still a little high, but there was nothing Sam could do about it now. Besides, where was Michael? He should have had his catcher's gear on by now.

Sam Douglas looked around and spotted his youngest son by the hot-dog cart. Even before a championship game! That kid was impossible!

"Michael!" his father shouted. "I told you to lay off the junk food!"

"It's okay, Dad," Tum Tum shouted back, pointing at a sign on the hot dog cart that said 100% MEAT. "These are *healthy* dogs! See?"

"Here you go," said the hot dog vendor, handing him two steaming franks on whole wheat buns. Tum Tum immediately started munching on one and put the other under his chest protector to save for later.

"By the way," he said, "do you know what time the ice cream guy gets here?"

"About half an hour, Mr. Health Nut," the vendor replied with a smirk.

"Perfect," Tum Tum said. He set the timer on his watch to beep in half an hour, in case he forgot. Then he headed toward the backstop. On the way, he saw a pretty girl with long blonde hair. It was Lisa DiMarino, Rocky's dream girl.

"Hi, Lisa." Tum Tum waved.

Lisa waved back, and Tum Tum smiled

to himself. The game was always more interesting when Lisa was around.

Up in the stands, Grandpa Mori sat with his daughter Jessica Douglas. Jessica was an attractive woman with short black hair and large brown eyes. She watched her sons proudly.

"Don't they look adorable in their uniforms, Dad?" she asked. "They're my three little Hall of Famers."

"Yeah," Mori replied good-naturedly. "The *Monster* Hall of Fame."

"Oh, come on, Dad, you don't really mean that," Jessica said, nudging him with her shoulder.

"Well," Mori replied, "let's just say they keep me young and make me old at the same time."

Above them in the bleachers, a speaker crackled to life as the game's announcer greeted the crowd: "Welcome to the final game of the league championship play-offs. Our series is tied at one game apiece, so this game will determine who goes home with the championship trophy: The Dragons . . . or the Mustangs!"

At the mention of each team's name, different parts of the crowd burst into cheers as parents and fans voiced their support for their teams.

"Play ball!" the umpire shouted.

Darren, the Mustangs pitcher and first hitter, got up to home plate and spit into the dirt. On the mound, Rocky got ready to pitch. Tum Tum was still munching on his first hot dog. Rocky threw the first pitch and Darren swung.

Crack! He popped the ball up into fair territory and sprinted toward first base.

"It's yours," Rocky shouted at Tum Tum.

Like a true catcher, Tum Tum charged forward and threw off his mask. Unfortunately, his hot dog went flying at the same time. Both the ball and the hot dog were in the air!

Tum Tum had to choose. After a split second, he dove and made a great catch.

Thud! A few feet away, the baseball fell to the ground.

A loud groan came from the crowd.

"Michael!" Sam Douglas shouted angrily from the dugout. "You're supposed to be playing baseball! Catch the ball, not the wiener!"

Tum Tum shrugged. Catching the hot dog hadn't been a conscious decision. He'd simply gone for the thing that meant the most to him. He took another bite of his hot dog, pulled down his catcher's mask, and got back behind the plate.

The next Mustangs batter got up to the plate. On the pitcher's mound, Rocky rocked and delivered.

Crack!

It was a grounder to the second baseman. It looked like an easy double-play. Colt dashed to second base. The second baseman fielded the grounder and tossed it toward him. As Colt prepared to catch it and throw to first for a double-play, he saw Darren barreling toward him. The Mustangs pitcher went into a slide, but he wasn't aiming at second base. He was aiming at Colt!

Colt jumped out of the way to avoid Darren's spikes. He bobbled the ball and didn't have time to throw to first.

"Safe!" the field umpire shouted. Darren stood up, smirking at Colt as he brushed the dirt off his uniform. Colt felt the blood rush to his face as he filled with anger and stomped over to Darren. The kid had tried to spike him!

The two boys stood toe-to-toe and face-to-face, each glaring at the other, each ready to fight.

"Want to do something about it?" Darren taunted.

"Yeah," Colt shot back.

"Okay, boys, break it up," the field umpire said, stepping between them. Darren smirked again. Colt went back to shortstop and tried to calm down.

Rocky managed to pitch his way out of the inning, giving up only one run. The Dragons got up to bat and scored four.

As the second inning began, a stocky Mustangs player named Keith got up to bat. Rocky hurled a fastball.

Crack! Keith smashed the ball into deep left center. Rocky grimaced. It looked like a home run, but the Dragons outfielder chased it down and managed to hold Keith to a triple. Now there were no outs and a man on third. The situation looked grim. As the next batter stepped up to the plate, Rocky knew he'd really have to buckle down if he was going to stop the Mustangs

from scoring any more runs. He looked
over at Tum Tum, who signaled for a curve-
ball. Rocky shook his head. Tum Tum signaled for a change-up. Rocky didn't want
to throw that, either.

"Get it together, Tum Tum," he
muttered.

"Rocky!" he heard Grandpa Mori shout
from the stands. "Concentration!"

His grandfather was right. He had to
concentrate. *Heart . . . mind . . . body . . .
uh . . .* Out of the corner of his eye he
caught a flash of blonde hair and turned to
look. It was Lisa! She gave him a dreamy
smile. *Lisa . . .*

Captivated by her smile, Rocky went
into a daze. Suddenly all his teammates on
the field looked like Lisa DiMarino. The
whole crowd looked like Lisa DiMarino,
and they were all chanting, "Rocky!
Rocky!" Even the Mustangs batter looked
like her. And she was giving him that soft
smile that he just couldn't resist.

Rocky went out of his pitching stance and
tossed the ball underhand to her. After all,
she was just a girl.

Crack! The Mustangs player smashed a

sacrifice drive right past Rocky's head. The center fielder caught it.

Tum Tum couldn't believe it. An *underhand* pitch? "Rocky!" he shouted. "This isn't softball!"

"Where's your head?" Sam Douglas called from the dugout. "Get your head in the game!"

Meanwhile, Keith had tagged up and was barreling in toward home. The Dragons center fielder heaved it at Tum Tum, who was covering the plate.

Pow! Keith and the baseball reached home plate at the same time.

"Ooof!" Tum Tum was knocked over backward as Keith scored, making it four to two in favor of the Dragons. Tum Tum reached into his chest protector and took out the squashed remains of the second hot dog. It looked pretty bad, but he thought maybe he could eat some of it.

Another Mustangs batter stepped up to the plate. Rocky threw the next pitch straight down the middle of the plate.

Ka-boom!

"That ball is going, going, gone!" shouted the announcer as the ball sailed over the right-field fence. Suddenly the score was tied, four to four.

Rocky managed to strike the next batter out and retire the side. Once again it was the Dragons turn to bat.

"At bat for the Dragons, Jeffrey Douglas," shouted the announcer.

Colt stepped up to the plate.

"Batter can't hit with a tree trunk!" the Mustang first baseman heckled.

"Yeah!" yelled the third baseman. "Come on batter, batter. Hey, batter, batter! Swing, batter!"

Colt could feel himself getting rattled. He had to try to stay cool. He had to try . . .

"Colt!" Grandpa Mori shouted from the stands. "Remember the bull's-eye!"

Colt turned and glared at him. Gerald, the Mustangs catcher, winked. Darren, the Mustangs pitcher, reared back and threw.

Whiff! Colt swung and missed.

"Strike one!" yelled the ump.

"Come on, Darren!" Gerald yelled. "This chump's got no stick. Blow it right by him!"

Colt felt his face burn.

"Yo, Colt," Gerald muttered in a taunting tone. "I hear you get mad pretty easy. You gettin' mad now?"

When Colt didn't respond, Gerald started making donkey noises. "Hee-haw, hee-haw. Gettin' mad, Colt?"

Colt spun around and started toward him.

"Hey!" shouted the home-plate ump, jumping between them. "None of that."

"Cool off, Colt!" Sam Douglas yelled from the dugout.

Colt got back into the batter's box and hunkered down for the next pitch. Darren let it go, and Colt took a big swing.

Whiff! Colt missed by a mile.

"Strike two!" yelled the ump.

Gerald smirked. Colt gritted his teeth and got ready for the next pitch. Little did he know that the catcher reached forward and pulled open the laces on his cleats.

"Hey, Colt, your shoe's untied," he said.

Colt looked down. "Time out, Ump."

The ump called time. Colt took off his batting helmet and kneeled down to retie his laces. When he wasn't looking, Gerald scooped up a handful of dirt and dropped it into the batting helmet.

When Colt finished tying his shoe, he straightened up and put the helmet back on. Dirt poured down his face.

"Ooops!" Gerald laughed. "How'd that happen? Someone put dirt in your helmet? That's 'cause you're a dirtbag, Colt."

That was it! Colt felt his blood boil. He threw down his bat and assumed an attack stance. He was going to teach this kid a lesson he'd never forget. . . .

"Colt!" Grandpa Mori shouted from the stands. "Control! Strength in restraint!"

Colt stepped back and tried to get control of his anger. But he was really ticked off. "Oh, Grandpa," he muttered to himself. "Back off already."

He picked up the bat and got ready for the next pitch. Darren rocked back and let it go . . . right at Colt's head!

Thunk! The ball smashed into Colt's batting helmet, knocking him to the ground. *That was it!* Colt leaped back to his feet. He was gonna kill that guy!

Crack! Colt snapped the bat in two over his knee and headed for the pitcher's mound.

"Jeffrey, stop!" his father shouted.

A split second later Colt felt someone tackle him around the ankles. As he went down, he saw that it was Gerald. Colt started wrestling him.

Mayhem broke out. Both teams rushed on the field and started fighting. The parents rushed out of the stands and started fighting. In the middle of it all, Tum Tum's watch started beeping.

"The ice cream man!" he gasped. Tum Tum ran off the field, quickly bought an ice cream sandwich, and ran back to rejoin the brawl.

Twenty minutes later, order had been restored. On the field — littered with bats, balls, mitts, batting helmets, and other baseball paraphernalia — the Dragons and the Mustangs lined up and faced each other. Both teams' uniforms were dirty, ripped, and disheveled. Behind each team stood their parents, whose clothes were equally dirty, ripped, and disheveled.

A glowering umpire stood between the two teams and lectured them.

"That was the most disgraceful display I've ever seen in a game," he shouted. "You are supposed to be learning to be citizens and sportsmen, not hooligans! I'm suspending this game for a week to give you a chance to cool down. We'll start the game over next Sunday. That is, *if* by then any of you decide to grow up!"

The parents winced and the kids flinched. Then the ump told them to go home.

Rocky, Colt, and Tum Tum trudged toward the dirt parking lot, where their parents and grandfather were loading baseball equipment into the family station wagon.

"How can we replay the game next Sunday?" Tum Tum asked, taking another bite from his ice-cream sandwich. "We'll be in Japan with Grandpa."

"We're not going to Japan," Colt grumbled. "We're staying here and playing baseball."

"What are you talking about?" Rocky asked in disbelief as they reached the car.

"Yeah, I want to go to Japan!" Tum Tum whined.

"I want to play ball!" Colt shot back.

Their father suddenly turned and glared

angrily at them. "I want! I want! Stop it! What's the matter with you? You call yourselves a team out there? You embarrassed yourselves and you made me ashamed."

Rocky and Tum Tum flinched at the sting in their father's words. But Colt stood up to him.

"How can I pay attention to the game with Grandpa pestering me from the stands like that?" he asked.

"Jeffrey!" his mother said in a scolding tone.

Rocky glanced at Grandpa Mori, who looked both surprised and hurt at being blamed by Colt.

"Well, you talk about what's embarrassing," Colt said. *"That's* embarrassing."

"That's enough, young man," his mother snapped.

Their father wasn't finished with his lecture.

"Michael, when are you going to learn that eating isn't the most important thing in the world, especially in the middle of a championship game?" he asked angrily. Next he turned to Rocky. "And you, Samuel. What were you looking at when you were supposed to be pitching?"

42

"And you, Jeffrey," his father said, turning to Colt. "Always getting into fights. How many times have we talked about that temper? How many times have I told you that you have to control it?"

Sam Douglas punctuated the question by angrily slamming the station wagon's gate closed.

"I wonder where he gets that temper from," the boys' mother said, rolling her eyes.

But Sam wasn't finished yet. Now he turned to Grandpa Mori. "You see what that ninja stuff does? All they want to do is fight."

Grandpa Mori didn't answer. He just looked down at the ground.

"Does this mean no Japan?" Tum Tum asked.

"It may mean no to a lot of things until you all decide to grow up."

Tum Tum shook his head slowly. "That stinks."

"Get in the car," Sam ordered.

The boys and their father got into the station wagon. Grandpa Mori and Jessica held back. Mori looked very disappointed. His daughter's heart went out to him.

"I'm sorry, Dad," she said in a low voice. Mori shrugged. "Four strands . . ."

"What?" Jessica wasn't sure she'd heard him correctly.

"I think our rope is beginning to unravel," Mori said sadly.

Chapter 5

It was the middle of the afternoon in downtown Los Angeles. In the dark, empty rock and roll club, chairs were piled on tables and a cleaning man pushed a broom across the floor. On the stage, three young musicians hovered over their instruments, getting ready to audition for a chance to play at the club. The bass player's name was Glam. He was of Japanese-American descent, with long, flowing, bleached-blond hair falling past his shoulders. The drummer, Slam, was stocky, with a heavy five-o'clock shadow on his jaw and a belly that crept out from under his black T-shirt. And that left Vinnie, the black leather-clad lead guitarist, whose greasy brown hair hung down to his shoulders.

The only other person in the club was the manager, a thin, nervous-looking man who chain-smoked cigarettes as he stood by the bar waiting for the band to play.

Up onstage, Glam plugged his bass into his amp. "Okay, dudes, ready to rock and roll?"

"Ready," said Slam.

"Uh, I think I'm ready," said Vinnie.

"Well, are you ready or not, dude?" Glam said.

"Well, uh, like, which did you say was, like, the E string, Glam?" Vinnie asked, looking down at his guitar.

Over by the bar, the club manager shook his head wearily. If it wasn't for the fact that Glam was the club's bartender, he wouldn't be wasting his time with these idiots.

"Dude, there are two E strings," Glam replied. "The one on the top and the one on the bottom."

"Wow," said Vinnie. "Two E strings? Do I have to play them both?"

"Play whatever you like, dude," Glam replied. "This is heavy metal."

"Right on!" shouted Slam. *Boom!* He whacked his drum.

"Okay, ready?" Glam yelled. "Uh-one, and uh-two, and uh-three!"

The band lurched into something thunderously loud that bore almost no resemblance to music. The three musicians furiously nodded their heads up and down, making their long hair fly as they battered their instruments and created something that sounded like a prolonged car crash.

"Stop!" the club's manager screamed as his ears throbbed painfully. "For God's sake, stop!"

No one onstage heard him. The manager grabbed the cleaning man. "You!" he shouted. "Go up there and pull the plug!"

The cleaning man ran onto the stage and pulled the plugs on the amps.

Whomp! Bang! Crash! The only sounds left were the banging of Slam's drums. Glam and Vinnie kept playing their dead guitars and thrashing their heads around, unaware that anything had changed.

After a while, Glam did notice something was wrong and looked up.

"Dudes," he said.

Whomp! Whomp! Slam kept smashing his drums. Vinnie kept playing his silent guitar.

"I said *'Dudes'!*" Glam shouted.

"Huh?" Vinnie looked up.

"Huh?" Slam looked up.

"The sound system's dead," Glam said.

"It is?" Vinnie looked puzzled.

"What'd you say the name of your band was?" the club's manager asked. All three musicians answered at the same time.

"Mondo Diarrhea," said Glam.

"Projectile Vomit," Slam said.

"Tough Noogies," said Vinnie.

Instantly the band members turned toward one another.

"I told you I didn't like that name, dude," Glam told Vinnie.

"I thought you guys said you'd go with Projectile Vomit this time," Slam whined.

"Guys, guys!" the club's manager shouted. "Shut up for a second, okay?"

"Uh, sure," Glam said. "So how'd you like it? I mean, before the sound went off?"

"Let me give you some career advice," the club's manager said. "You stink. Anything you don't understand about that? The 'you' part? The 'stink' part?"

"Well, like sometimes people say that as a compliment," Slam said.

"Not this time," the club's manager said. "Listen, Glam, get behind the bar and be the bartender. Remember, that's what I hired you for, okay? And you two other dirtbags can get out of my club."

Glam's shoulders slumped as he turned to his fellow musicians. "I told you we should have rehearsed."

The guys climbed down from the stage and followed Glam to the bar.

"I gotta make some money," Vinnie said.

"Me, too," said Slam.

"Well, get a job like I did, dudes," Glam told them as he ducked under the bar.

"A job?" Vinnie screwed up his face.

"We need money bad," Slam said, "but not *that* bad."

"Oh, yeah." The manager interrupted them. "Glam, there's a phone call for you."

Glam went behind the bar and picked up the receiver. He recognized the voice right away. It was his uncle Koga, calling from

Japan to ask if Glam had received the Federal Express envelope he'd sent.

"You guys see a Fed Ex envelope around here?" Glam asked his buddies.

"There's one," Slam said, pointing to a trash can down at the end of the bar. A white-blue-and-orange Fed Ex envelope was sticking out.

Vinnie got it and gave it to Glam, who ripped it open. Two photographs slid out. One was of some old Japanese dude. The other was an old dagger with an etched blade.

"Cool knife," Glam said into the phone.

Uncle Koga started talking. Glam listened, nodding every so often. When he hung up the phone, he was grinning. "Dudes," he said to Vinnie and Slam, "I think I just found out how we can make some money."

The boys were back in their grandfather's cabin. Tum Tum and Rocky were in the kitchen, preparing dinner. Rocky was filling a large pot with water, while Tum Tum, using a ninja sword, chopped a tomato, a cucumber, and a head of lettuce for a salad. Colt was sitting off by himself, trying to flip playing cards into a hat.

Grandpa Mori came into the room and looked over at Rocky, who had opened a cookbook and was squinting into it. "Put on your glasses, Rocky."

Rocky looked up. "Do I *have* to?"

"You know you need them when you read," his grandfather said.

"But girls think they're dorky," Rocky complained.

"Yeah," Tum Tum agreed. "And who ever heard of a four-eyed ninja?"

"Put them on, Rocky," Grandpa Mori ordered.

Rocky reluctantly took a pair of glasses out of the side pocket of his ninja bag and slid them on. Grandpa Mori nodded and smiled.

"Better a ninja with glasses than a ninja with a seeing-eye dog," he said. He nodded toward Colt. "What is with your brother?"

Rocky looked over at Colt. The kid had been in a bad mood ever since the baseball game.

"Hey," Rocky called to him. "You don't help, you don't eat."

"Fine with me," Colt replied with a shrug. "I'm not hungry anyway."

Rocky glanced back at his grandfather and raised his eyebrows as if to say, "I don't know what's bugging him."

The phone rang, and Grandpa Mori answered it. "Hello? Oh, yes, I've been expecting your call. How many tickets? I'm not sure. Can you hold a moment?"

He put his hand over the phone and turned toward the boys. "It's the travel agent. I have to tell her how many tickets for Japan."

"Get one for me!" Tum Tum cried.

"No," said Colt.

"I'm going!" Tum Tum yelled at him.

"No way," replied Colt.

"You have to decide, boys," their grandfather said. "I have to tell the travel agent."

"Okay, guys," Rocky said. "We have to decide."

The three boys huddled.

"How can we not go?" Tum Tum asked in a low voice.

"He's right," Rocky told Colt. "It's Japan. How often do we get a chance like this? You really want to throw it away?"

"What about winning the baseball championship?" Colt asked. "You really want to throw *that* away?"

"Let's vote on it," Tum Tum said. "I want to go to Japan. What about you, Rocky?"

"Forget it," Colt said. "Your vote doesn't count."

"Does too," Tum Tum insisted.

"Does not," Colt shot back.

"Cool it, guys," Rocky cautioned them.

"Look, Rocky," Colt said. "You could pitch the winning game. You could win the championship for us. What do you think Lisa DiMarino would think of that?"

Rocky had been certain he wanted to go to Japan. He didn't think Colt could come up with a good reason for him not to go. But then again, he hadn't taken Lisa into consideration. Colt was right. If he shut out the Mustangs with great pitching, he'd be the game's hero. Lisa would love that.

Tum Tum saw the glazed, fuzzy look in Rocky's eyes. It was the look he always got when he thought about his latest lady love.

"Oh, no, Rocky!" Tum Tum gasped. "You're not gonna change your mind, are you?"

"Ahem." Across the room, Mori cleared his throat. "The travel agent is waiting. I have to tell her if you're going to Japan or not."

Colt gave Rocky a questioning look. Rocky looked down at the ground.

"You tell him," Colt whispered.

"No, *you* tell him," Rocky whispered back.

"I'll tell him," Tum Tum volunteered. "Grandpa, we voted, and we decided we're all going to go to Jap — "

Colt clamped his hand around Tum Tum's mouth.

"We decided we're going to stay here and play baseball," Colt said.

Grandpa Mori gazed down sadly at the ground for a moment, then turned back to the phone and spoke to the travel agent. "Just one ticket, please. Yes, I'll put it on my credit card. Yes, I'll come pick it up right now."

Without a word Grandpa Mori walked over to his blue ninja bag and took his wallet out of the side pocket. The boys watched in silence as he headed for the door. Suddenly Tum Tum jumped up and ran after him.

"Grandpa!" he called.

Grandpa Mori stopped. "Yes?"

"I just want you to know that I voted to go with you."

Grandpa Mori smiled wistfully and patted the boy on his head. "I'm proud of you, Tum Tum. You want to continue your ninja training."

"Ninja?" Tum Tum shook his head. "To tell you the truth, Grandpa, I really wanted to learn to be a sumo wrestler."

Grandpa Mori's eyebrows rose in surprise. "You, a sumo wrestler?"

"Sure, why not?" Tum Tum asked.

Grandpa Mori didn't know what to say. "I think a better question is, why?"

"Well, I saw a TV show about them," Tum Tum explained. "You should see how much those guys get to eat everyday."

Grandpa Mori sighed and shook his head. His grandsons were young. They had so much to learn. "All right, boys. Don't burn dinner, and clean up this mess."

"Don't worry, Grandpa," Tum Tum assured him. "By the time you get back, this place will be spotless."

Not far away, a dented old green pickup truck with a camper turned up the road that led to grandpa Mori's cabin. Spare tires and emergency water cans were lashed to its sides, and deer antlers were nailed to the roof of the cab where the driver sat. Inside, the camper was filled with amps, guitars, and other rock and roll equipment. Slam was driving. Glam and Vinnie sat next to him in the cab. They were eating french fries from white paper bags, and slurping milk shakes, as Metallica thundered out of the pick-up's speakers.

"Hey, dudes, I was thinking," Glam said.

"Really?" Vinnie looked at him, amazed.

"Yeah, really," Glam insisted. "And I came up with a new name for the band, dudes."

"Mucous and the Membranes?" Slam asked.

"No. Raw Teenage Acne," Glam said.

"Yeah, we could call our first album *Pus Full of Zits*," Slam said.

"Or like, *Zits Full of Pus!*" exclaimed Vinnie.

"Yeah, I like that better," said Slam.

An old Toyota was coming down the road toward them. As it passed Glam shouted, "Stop!"

Crunch! Crunch!

Slam hit the brakes so hard that Glam and Vinnie lurched and smashed into the windshield.

"Whoa, like, pain," Vinnie groaned, holding his forehead.

"How come you stopped so hard, dude?" Glam asked as he massaged his face where it had hit the windshield.

"You said stop," Slam explained.

"Yeah, Glam," said Vinnie. "Like, why'd you say it anyway?"

" 'Cause I think it was him!" Glam said.

"Who?"

Glam took the photograph of Grandpa Mori out of the envelope. "The old guy, dudes." He took the picture of the dagger out. "The one we're stealing *this* from."

For the first time Slam actually saw a picture of the dagger. "Whoa. No wonder your uncle's paying us twenty grand to steal it. That's a nice letter opener."

57

"Yeah, but, like, twenty grand, man," said Vinnie skeptically. "That's a lot of cash. You think it's *that* hard to find a letter opener in Japan?"

"Well, maybe there's a law against them over there or something," Slam speculated.

"Oh, yeah." Vinnie nodded. "Like an antiletter-opener law or something."

"So you gotta smuggle them in," Slam said.

"Dudes, dudes," Glam said. "Who cares why my uncle wants it? Just think about all that money, and the fact that the old guy's gone. You know what that means?"

"He went to the mall?" Vinnie guessed.

"Or maybe to the 7-Eleven?" Slam guessed.

"It means his cabin's empty, dudes!" Glam grinned.

Slam stared at Vinnie, who stared at Glam. Then all together they shouted, "Rock and roll!"

Chapter 6

Inside the cabin, the boys quietly started to clean up the kitchen. Nobody spoke. The mood was gloomy. Rocky was washing pots at the sink. Nearby, Colt was sweeping the kitchen floor.

"You're really being a jerk to Grandpa," Rocky told him.

"Me?" Colt looked surprised. "You wanted to stay, too."

"Sometimes I think you don't even want to be a ninja anymore," Tum Tum told Colt as he brought some dishes to the sink.

"I never said that," Colt answered. He

was just about to explain how important he thought the baseball game was when . . .

Buuuzzzzzz . . . The mask alarm on the wall started to buzz and flash. Rocky stared up at it, quickly drying his hands with a dish towel.

"Somebody's coming," he said.

"Maybe robbers," Colt gasped.

"Or maybe someone's lost," said Tum Tum.

"Ninjas should always be prepared for battle," Rocky said, crossing through the living room. "Or to give directions."

Colt and Tum Tum followed him to the window. Outside, they saw the beat-up old pick-up truck and camper rumble to a stop in front of the cabin. Three large, grungy guys climbed out of the mobile home.

"Hey, like, know what I was thinking?" Vinnie said as he and the others stretched after the long ride.

"No, what, dude?" Glam said.

"Well, like, I know why we're going in there," Vinnie said. "But, like, as long as we're there, let's bag any hardware we see, okay?"

"You mean, like CD players, speakers, TVs?" Slam asked. "That kind of hardware?"

"You got it, man." Vinnie grinned and nodded.

"Whoa, what a slammin' idea!" Slam said.

"Yeah, dude," Glam said, giving Vinnie a high hard-knuckle five. "It's times like this that I realize what a deep thinker you really are."

"So what's the plan?" Slam asked.

Vinnie and Glam gave each other vacant looks. "Plan?"

"Yeah, like how're we gonna do it?" Slam asked.

Vinnie scratched his head. "Whoa, like, we never thought about that."

Glam rubbed his chin. "I know! We'll break in!"

"Slammin'!" cried Slam.

"But what'll we use?" Glam asked.

Once again the grungers looked puzzled.

"Hey, wait a minute!" Vinnie snapped his fingers and climbed back into the truck. Pulling open the glove compartment, he took out a metal spatula.

Glam shook his head. "I don't think so, dude."

Vinnie frowned and rummaged around the front seat. He found an old black leather boot with metal studs. "How about this?"

"Good for stomping heads, man, not breaking into cabins," said Slam.

Vinnie came up with a screwdriver next.

"I think you're getting closer, dude," said Glam.

Vinnie looked around the pick-up. "Like, that's all there is, dudes. I mean, the only other thing is this long metal crowbar."

"Bummer," Slam said, shaking his head.

"What are we gonna do?" Vinnie asked.

"Guess we'll have to try the crowbar," said Glam with a shrug. "I mean, what choice do we have?"

Vinnie picked up the crowbar and hopped out of the truck.

"Okay, you guys do the deed," Glam said. "I'll keep a lookout."

Meanwhile, inside the cabin, the boys had heard the entire conversaiton.

"Directions?" Colt asked, looking at his brothers.

"I don't think so," they all said simultaneously.

Rocky glanced over at Colt. "You with us?"

Colt responded with a nod and the thumbs-up sign. Tum Tum was glad to see that Colt was still into ninja.

"Let's murderlize 'em," he whispered hoarsely.

The boys quickly ran into their bedrooms and changed into their ninja outfits. Each was formulating a battle plan in his mind.

Moments later, Rocky headed up to the attic and climbed out on the roof, carrying a thin spool of wire. Downstairs, Colt pulled on sweatpants and a sweatshirt over his ninja outfit. The sweats were the same red-and-blue pattern as the quilt on his bed.

In the kitchen, Tum Tum pulled open the refrigerator. "Let's see what we have for our guests," he mused, taking out a dozen eggs, a can of whipped cream, and a banana-cream pie. He carried them all into the pantry and shut the door. Inside, he tied his ninja belt to the doorknob, then took a warm can of soda from the shelf and started shaking it with a mischievous grin.

Vinnie and Slam reached the front door

of the cabin. They wedged the crowbar into the doorway and started to lean on it.

"Okay, man," Vinnie groaned. "Let's give it the old heave-ho! On three. One, two . . ."

Above them on the roof, Rocky whispered, "Three!" to himself and pulled on the wire. What he knew, that the grungers didn't, was that the wire was attached to the inside of the front door, and when Rocky pulled, the door opened.

"*Ahhhhhhh!*" The grungers screamed as the door flew open and they sailed inside.

Crash! Vinnie crashed into the kitchen counter and sank to the floor.

Ripp! Slam's head smashed through the seat of a cane chair. The grunger staggered to his feet with the chair on his head and tried to pull it off. He stumbled sideways and stepped on Vinnie's hand.

"*Oww!*" Vinnie shouted. "Get offa me!"

"Sorry, dude." Slam yanked the chair off his head.

"I guess that crowbar worked, man," Vinnie said, getting to his feet.

"I'll say," Slam agreed. "Never thought of using one of those to break into houses, but hey, from now on!"

"Right on, dude!" Vinnnie and Slam happily banged heads.

"So now what?" Vinnie asked.

"Well, look!" Slam pointed at an old wooden desk across the room. "A desk!"

"So?" Vinnie said.

"So, if you were going to hide a letter opener, wouldn't you put it in there?" Slam asked.

"Devious!" Vinnie gasped.

The two grungers hurried over to the desk and started going through the drawers.

"Found it!" Slam gasped, holding up a plain letter opener. "Let's go!"

He started toward the door, but Vinnie grabbed him by the collar.

"Hold it, man," Vinnie snapped. "Were you hatched from a moron egg? Look." He took out the photo of the dagger. "Does that look like this?"

Slam looked at the letter opener in his hand and compared it to the dagger. "No."

"Then that's not it," Vinnie said.

"You really think Glam's uncle will know the difference?" Slam asked.

"I don't know, man," Vinnie said. "But there's twenty thousand bucks on the line,

so why take a chance? Here, you keep this."
He handed Slam the photo of the dagger.
"You look around down here. I'll go
upstairs."

Slam went over to the kitchen and
started going through the drawers there,
carefully comparing the knives, potato
peelers, and whisks to the photo. None of
them seemed to be exactly what he was
looking for, but he wanted to make sure.

Upstairs, Vinnie went down a hall and
into a kid's bedroom. There were posters
of basketball players on the walls and
model airplanes hanging from the ceiling.
He sat down on a bed covered with a red-
and-blue quilt and started to look through
the drawers of a dresser beside it.

Back downstairs, Slam finished going
through the kitchen drawers. No dagger
there. Looking around, he noticed the door
to the pantry. He figured he better check
what was inside, but the door seemed
stuck. Slam gave it a harder pull. Suddenly
the door flew open and he was hit in the
face with a spray of foamy warm root beer.

Bang! The door slammed shut again.

"Hey!" Slam shouted. "What the . . .?"

He grabbed a dish towel and wiped the soda off his face. Then, more carefully this time, he slowly opened the pantry door and peeked inside.

Crack! Crack! Crack! A dozen eggs smashed rapid-fire into his face. Slam reeled backward as yolks, egg whites, and shells dripped down his face and onto the floor.

Now he was mad! Slam wiped the gunk away with his hands and yanked open the door.

"Oooooofff!" Something smashed him in the stomach. It was Tum Tum's head, as the boy launched himself into the grunger like a human missile.

Bonk! Slam flew backward against the kitchen counter, then bounced back toward the pantry and . . .

Splat! A cream pie smacked into his face. Slam's entire face was now covered with white whipped cream, pie filling, and crust. He stopped and licked his lips. "Wow, lemon meringue."

"Banana-cream, bozo," Tum Tum informed him. "Nice try."

It suddenly occurred to Slam that there

were other people in the house. *"Vinnie!"* he cried.

Upstairs, Vinnie had been listening to the shouting and commotion. At first he thought maybe Slam had found the dagger, but now he wasn't so sure.

"Vinnie," Slam was shouting. *"The house ain't empty!"*

Ain't empty? Vinnie frowned.

"What are you talkin' about?" he shouted back. "There's nobody here!"

The words were hardly out of his mouth when Colt rose up behind him. Vinnie jumped up and turned around. What was this? Some kid wearing clothes that matched the bedspread?

"KEIIIII!" Colt whooped and landed a kick in the middle of Vinnie's chest, sending him backward out the door and thudding down the stairs.

"Oof! Uh! Unh! Ow! Huh?" Vinnie rolled backward down the stairs and hit the floor. Colt slid down the banister after him.

Dazed and confused, Vinnie staggered to his feet just in time to see the soles of Colt's tennis shoes heading right for his face.

"*Yikes!*" Vinnie ducked and cowered, expecting to get smashed any second.

But nothing happened.

Vinnie blinked and straightened up. The kid had vanished. It was a miracle!

Then someone tapped him on his shoulder. Vinnie turned around.

POW! A foot smacked into his head, knocking him flat on his back.

Colt stood over the prostrate grunger. The imprint from the bottom of his tennis shoe was rising, swollen and red, from the guy's forehead.

"Awesome!" Colt said with a grin.

"Hey, Colt!" Tum Tum shouted.

Colt crossed over to the kitchen, where Tum Tum was following another grunger around with a can of whipped cream. Every time Slam managed to wipe some whipped cream away from his eyes, Tum Tum sprayed him again.

"I'm making a dork sundae," Tum Tum explained to his brother as he sprayed Slam some more. "Ooops! Missed a spot!"

Tum Tum ducked under Slam and shot some whipped cream up his nose.

"*Arrrghh!*" Slam staggered backward,

groping for something to hold on to. He grabbed the door of one of the kitchen cabinets and tried to pull himself up. At the same moment, Vinnie stumbled toward him.

Crunk! The cabinet came partway off the wall.

Crash! Bang! Clang! Dozens of dishes, pots, and pans poured out of the cabinet, crashing over Slam and Vinnie and knocking them to the kitchen floor.

The two dazed grungers lay in a heap on the kitchen floor, covered with broken dishes, pots, and pans. Slam's face was still covered with whipped cream. Tum Tum stood over him, trying to decide on a finishing touch. Suddenly it came to him. He reached for a jar on the kitchen counter and took out a cherry, placing it right between Slam's eyes.

"Perfect!" he shouted. "A grunge-cream pie!"

Outside, Glam was getting bored, waiting for his buddies to find the dagger. He turned the pick-up's side-view mirror out and fluffed his long silver-blond hair. Then he flexed his muscles and struck various poses. Finally he played some air guitar, pretending he was onstage in some radical place . . . like maybe Cleveland.

Glam finished his air guitar performance and raised a triumphant fist in the air.

Rocky was perched above him, hidden in the branches of a dense green pine tree, watching. What a jerk, he thought as he dropped a pinecone.

Plink! The pinecone hit Glam in the head and bounced to the ground. Glam looked around, but didn't see anything.

Ploink! Rocky sent another pinecone down onto Glam's head.

"Huh? What's going on?" Glam jumped around and tried to peer up into the tree. "Who's up there?"

Rocky didn't answer. Glam picked up a stick from the ground and turned in circles, not knowing where the next attack would come from.

"Up here, grunge breath!" Rocky shouted. "Yeah, I mean you, Metallica head."

Glam looked up at the tree just as Rocky sent a dozen more pinecones raining down on him.

Plink! Ploink! Plunk! Glam raised his

arms to ward off the attack of the pinecones.

"Who are you?" Glam shouted. "Come down here!"

When Rocky didn't answer, Glam turned to the cabin and yelled, "Vinnie! Slam!"

They didn't answer, either. "Where are those dudes?" Glam wondered, and started toward the cabin to find out.

Inside the cabin, Vinnie and Slam slowly stood up, brushing off the broken plates, pots, and pans. Slam grabbed a dish towel and wiped off the pie filling and whipped cream. Not far away, Tum Tum and Colt stood by the front door.

"Oh, please, Mr. Man," Tum Tum called in a taunting voice. "Please don't hurt us!"

Vinnie and Slam looked at each other. They shared one common desire: *Kill those kids!*

"Get 'em!" Vinnie shouted. He and Slam lunged toward the kids. Unfortunately, they didn't know that Colt and Tum Tum had covered the floor with salad oil and whipped cream.

"*Whoops!*" Vinnie and Slam cried at the same time as they went sliding toward

the door. At the last second, Colt pushed
the door open and Vinnie and Slam slid
right into . . . Glam!

Thwomp! Vinnie and Slam knocked
Glam backward into the yard, where they
all fell into a heap. Tum Tum and Colt stood
near them, laughing.

"Who are you guys?" Vinnie groaned as
he and the other grungers struggled to
their feet. "The two midget mutants?"

"Not!" Rocky replied, swinging out of
the tree toward them.

Wham! Rocky's feet slammed into their
faces, knocking them all flat on their
backs.

Rocky landed next to his brothers and
together they said, "We're the three
ninjas."

The brothers ran off in different directions. With groans and moans, the grungers rose slowly to their feet.

"You dudes find the dagger?" Glam
asked.

Slam and Vinnie shook their heads.

"Well, get back into that cabin," Glam
said.

Again, the other two shook their heads.

There was no way they were going back in there.

"Aw, you wusses," Glam muttered and headed for the cabin. He stepped inside and immediately hit the oil and whipped cream.

"*Yahhhh!*" *Crunch!* Glam flew up into the air, hit the wall, and smashed face first into the floor. He staggered to his feet and looked around. "Now, if I were a dagger, where would I be?"

As Glam looked around, Tum Tum secretly slid one end of a rope out the cabin door to Colt. With the other end he made a noose, and then tiptoed up behind the platinum-blond grunger.

Glam was standing on the rug in the living room. Tum Tum grabbed it and yanked.

"*Ahhh!*" *Whomp!* Once again Glam flew up in the air, slammed in the wall, and came down hard on the floor. But this time the force of the impact knocked both the picture on the wall and the panel behind it askew, revealing Grandpa Mori's secret compartment, and the dagger hidden within. As Glam got up he found himself staring at the dagger!

Outside, Vinnie and Slam had lost interest in the dagger.

"Let's get out of here while we're still standing!" Slam shouted. He and Vinnie raced to the pick-up and jumped in, so eager to flee that they didn't notice the end of the rope Colt had tied to the bumper.

In the driver's seat, Slam gunned the engine and threw the truck into gear.

Meanwhile, back in the cabin, Glam was just about to get to his feet when he felt a rope go around his ankle. Looking back over his shoulder, he saw Tum Tum tightening the noose.

"Come see us again sometime," Tum Tum said with a smile.

"*Hellllpppppp!*" The next thing Glam knew he was pulled straight out of the house as the pick-up truck took off.

"We'll keep the lights on!" Tum Tum stood at the door and waved.

Slam floored the pick-up truck. "Those were the toughest runts I've ever dealt with."

"There were a million of them," Vinnie agreed. "They were all over the place."

The pick-up got halfway down the driveway, then Slam hit the brakes.

"What's wrong?" Vinnie gasped.

"We forgot Glam!" Slam yelled.

But not for long. The pick-up truck and camper might have stopped, but the force of Glam's momentum kept him going . . . .

Crack! Glam smashed face first into the rear window of the camper. He crumpled onto the ground in a heap.

"Glam's here," Vinnie said to Slam. "Now drive!"

A little later, Grandpa Mori returned from the travel agent's office. As he stepped into the cabin, the boys slid excitedly down the banister. Mori couldn't believe what he was seeing. His cabin was a wreck! The floor was covered with oil and whipped cream, the plates were smashed, the pots and pans dented, the furniture was broken.

Mori turned to his grandsons. "This is spotless?"

The boys all spoke at once: "There were three bad guys! They wanted to rob the cabin! We got rid of them!"

Grandpa Mori saw the spot where the picture on the wall had been pushed aside and the secret panel knocked out. The dagger was revealed. "What were they trying to steal?"

"They just wanted TVs and stuff," Colt said. "We heard them talking."

The other boys nodded in support. Grandpa Mori said nothing. He went over to the wall and replaced the loose panel.

"We really took care of them, Grandpa," Rocky said proudly. "You should have seen it."

"Yeah," said Tum Tum. "They finally gave up and ran away."

"This place is a mess," their grandfather said tersely.

It was clear that he was not pleased. The boys were caught off guard.

"But, Grandpa," Colt said. "We used everything you taught us. We were great."

The creases deepened in Mori's forehead. "A true ninja does not brag about his skills," he said disapprovingly. He focused on Colt. "But I forgot, *you* don't want any more advice from me."

Colt and his brothers stood slack-jawed. No one knew what to say.

"Next time, call the police," Grandpa

Mori said, shaking his head sadly. "Now get this mess cleaned up. Then start packing. Your parents will be here tomorrow morning to take you home."

Mori left the room. His grandsons watched in silence, feeling terrible.

Chapter 7

That night the grungers' pick-up stopped
beside a phone booth at a gas station. Glam
got out and, using a stolen telephone credit
card, dialed his uncle in Japan.

Halfway around the world, Koga, the
man in black, picked up the phone.
"Nephew, do you have the dagger?" he
asked.

"Uh, not exactly, Uncle," Glam said.

"Not exactly?" Koga repeated. "What
does that mean?"

"Well, there were security guards and
dogs," Glam said.

"I don't care about security guards and

dogs," Koga snapped impatiently. "Now I ask you again. Do you have the dagger?"

"Well, I saw it," Glam said. "I mean, I got real close to it. But, uh, it's not like it's actually in my hands."

"I see," Koga said tersely.

"But I'll try again, Uncle," Glam said nervously.

"I want that dagger in my hands immediately," Koga growled into the phone. "Get the dagger and be at my office here in Tokyo, or you will receive nothing, understand?"

"Uh, yeah, loud and clear." Glam hung up and turned to Vinnie and Slam, who were using the crowbar to jimmy open the Pepsi machine next to the phone booth.

"What'd he say?" Vinnie asked.

"No dagger, no money," replied Glam.

"I got an idea!" Slam said. "Suppose we make a fake dagger and bring him that?"

Glam and Vinnie glared at him. Slam shrugged. "Well, it was just an idea."

"Every time you have an idea, the room smells for ten minutes," Glam said sourly. "The only way we're gonna get the moola is if we deliver the real dagger."

*   *   *

The next morning, the Douglases came to get their three sons. Jessica and Sam stood on the front porch of the cabin with Colt and Rocky while Grandpa Mori loaded his bags into the family station wagon.

"How come Grandpa's putting his bags in the car?" Rocky asked.

"We're taking him to the airport on our way home," Jessica said. "I think he's really disappointed that you're not going to Tokyo with him."

"Well, I don't think it's so bad," Sam Douglas said. "Everything they need to know about life, they can learn on the baseball field." He nodded toward Colt. "You're going to play like one of the team next week, right? No more fighting?"

"Right," Colt replied.

"Because there's no place for that out on the field," his father said.

"I said right," Colt replied irritably. "You want me to sing 'Take Me Out to the Ball Game,' too?"

"No!" Sam shot back. "What I want is an end to this attitude."

Colt rolled his eyes. Meanwhile, his father glanced over at the car, where Mori was packing. Then Sam Douglas turned back to his two oldest sons.

"It'll be good for you boys to be away from this ninja stuff for a while," he said in a low voice, then started toward the car.

"What a pain," Colt muttered.

"Now don't forget," his mother said. "Your dad was a kid once, too."

"No way." Colt shook his head. "He was born full grown, with a briefcase."

"That's enough," Jessica said. "Now go get in the car." She turned back toward the front door and called inside. "Come on, Michael, we're all waiting for you."

Up in his room, Tum Tum was transferring his stash of candy into his blue ninja bag. First came a bag of sugar-free jelly beans. Then a box of all-natural licorice sticks. Then the Ding Dongs, the beef jerkies, and his karate suit. Tum Tum glanced around furtively to make sure no one was peeking, then brought out the "good stuff," including his cherished jumbo-size chocolate bar.

"Huh!" Tum Tum gasped in horror. Half of the chocolate bar wrapper was empty!

Someone had been filching the good stuff! Tum Tum glanced around and spotted a mousetrap in a corner of the room. A smile came to his lips as he picked it up, forced it open, and put it in his bag. This'll fix the next guy who steals my candy, he thought.

"Come on, Michael!" he heard his mother call from outside. But as Tum Tum ran down the stairs and out the front door, he passed Grandpa Mori coming back in.

"Where are you going?" Tum Tum asked.

"I almost forgot the most important thing," Mori replied, going into the cabin.

A moment later he came back carrying the dagger and showed it to Jessica and Sam before packing it into his bag.

Not far away, the grungers' pick-up truck was parked on the side of the road. In a feeble attempt to camouflage it, the grungers had thrown some tree limbs and foliage around it. Glam sat in the truck, watching the activity outside Mori's cabin with binoculars. Slam and Vinnie sat beside him. Slam was banging out drumrolls on the dashboard with his sticks.

"Hey, dudes!" Glam said. "They're leaving in the station wagon, and they're taking the dagger with them."

Vinnie turned to Slam. "We'd better follow them!"

"Right!" Slam turned on the engine and hit the gas and the truck peeled out.

Hardly anyone talked on the way to the airport. The boys felt bad that Grandpa Mori was going to Japan alone, but Colt and Rocky were still torn between that and the big baseball game. At the Air Japan terminal, they all got out of the car and watched while Sam reached in the back for Mori's blue ninja bag.

"Which of these bags is yours, Mori?" Sam asked as cars pulled up around them and travelers laden with suitcases and garment bags hopped out.

"That one," Mori said, pointing to one of the bags.

"Here you go." Sam handed him the bag. Mori hardly glanced at it. He was preoccupied with other thoughts and turned to the boys.

"Good-bye, boys," he said with a heavy heart. "I wish you were coming with me."

Colt and Rocky stared down at the sidewalk, unable to look their grandfather in the eye. Tum Tum ran to Mori and threw his arms around him.

"I wish I was coming, too, Grandpa," he said, looking back angrily at his brothers. "Lamebrains."

Colt and Rocky shared a guilty glance while Jessica hugged her father.

"Okay, everyone," Sam said, checking his watch. "Let's get back in the car. Grandpa Mori has to catch his plane."

The Douglas family got back into the car and waved one last time. Grandpa Mori stood on the sidewalk and waved back sadly. The station wagon pulled back into traffic. With a sigh Mori watched it go, then turned and walked into the terminal.

He was just going through the sliding glass doors when the grungers' pick-up screeched up to the curb.

"He's got the bag!" Glam yelled, pointing.

"What do you think he's doing?" Slam asked.

"Well, he's at the airport," Vinnie said. "You think he's gonna take a plane somewhere?"

"That must be it!" Glam snapped his fingers. "Come on, dudes!"

"But where do you think he's going?" Slam asked.

"Doesn't matter, man," Vinnie said, pulling open the door. "Wherever it is, we're going, too."

"How?" Slam asked. "We don't have any money."

Glam reached into his pocket and took out a handful of brightly colored credit cards. "Maybe, but we've got lots of stolen credit cards, dudes!"

Almost a day later, the three grungers found themselves crowded into a small rented car and chasing a black-and-white cab carrying Mori through heavy Tokyo traffic.

"Far out, man!" Slam shouted as he drove. "We're in Japan!"

Beep! Beep! Angry Japanese drivers appeared to be driving straight at them and shaking their fists.

"Why's everyone being so rude, dudes?" Glam asked.

"Yeah, and how come everyone's driving

on the wrong side of the road?" Vinnie asked from the back.

Screech! Car after car skidded out of their way.

"Know what, dudes?" Glam said. "I've got a feeling *they're* not on the wrong side of the road. *We* are."

"Watch out!" Vinnie shouted. A truck was bearing down on them.

Slam spun the wheel, and the car skidded over to the other side of the road.

"Oh, wow!" Slam gasped. "Glam's right. They do it backward here. All the cars on this side of the road should be going the other way."

"Just get behind the cab with the old dude," Glam said.

The black-and-white cab turned the corner. Slam followed, right into oncoming traffic again.

"Wrong side!" Glam shouted, raising his hands to protect his face.

Screech! Slam spun the wheel, and they narrowly missed a head-on collision.

"Pay attention!" Vinnie yelled.

"I can't help it," Slam replied. "I'm not used to this."

"Don't lose him, man," Vinnie said.

"How am I gonna lose him?" Slam asked. "In this traffic I can't even get close to him."

"Man, there sure are a lot of Japanese restaurants here," Vinnie said, pointing at the sushi bars in the buildings lining the streets around them.

"Yeah, that's a weird thing about Japan," Glam said, rolling his eyes. He pointed ahead. "Look, he's turning again."

Slam followed and once again turned right into oncoming traffic.

"Wrong side! Wrong side!" Glam and Vinnie both screamed.

Slam spun the wheel and swerved back into the left lane.

Crash! They smashed into the back of Mori's cab, which had stopped.

Thunk! Glam smacked his head against the windshield.

"I gotta stop doing that," he groaned, holding his head.

"Hey, look!" Slam pointed through the windshield. The trunk of the cab had popped open, and Mori's luggage and ninja bag were visible.

"Open season on luggage!" Glam shouted and pushed open the door of the rental car.

The grungers jumped out of their car and rushed around to the back of the taxi. Vinnie reached into the cab's trunk and yanked out the ninja bag. The others took Mori's luggage. The three grungers started to run.

"Hey!" In the back of the cab, Mori saw the grungers steal his things. He tried to jump out of the cab to chase them but as he moved, he became dizzy and his vision blurred. The traffic on the street outside the cab seemed to spin in front of Mori's eyes . . . then everything went black.

Not long after that, the grungers raced into a tall black building and rode the elevator to the uppermost floor. They jumped out of the elevator and burst through the doors into Koga's office and into the private gym adjoining it. Koga was jogging on a treadmill. A man wearing a white suit and a black shirt stood next to him, holding a towel and a pitcher of water on a tray.

"Greetings, Uncle," Glam said, bowing.

Koga glanced at him impassively.

"Uh, we did your bidding. We got the goods right here." Glam expected Koga to smile, but his uncle didn't.

"I was expecting you earlier," Koga said.

Slam had been looking around nervously at the other men in the room. Besides Koga and the man wearing the white suit, there were two huge sumo-type dudes in striped suits. Slam turned to Koga.

"Look, man, I don't know if you know this or not," he said, "but everybody in your country drives on the wrong side of the road. Like, I was making this turn and — "

"Quiet, fool!" Koga snapped.

"Hey, who are you to call me a fool?" Slam asked.

Koga snapped his fingers. "Ishikawa!"

The dude in the white suit stepped ominously toward Slam, and the two monster sumo-dudes followed.

"Know what?" Slam said in a trembling voice. "You can call me fool any time you like. Fool Slam or Slam Fool. Whichever you prefer."

Koga ignored him and reached toward Glam. "Give it to me," he said.

Glam gestured to Vinnie. "Behold! The dagger of doom!" He nodded at Vinnie, who opened the blue bag and stuck his hand in.

Snap!

"*Ahhhh!*" Vinnie screamed and yanked his hand out. He started jumping up and down, shaking his hand. A mousetrap was clamped down on his fingers.

Glam and Slam put their hands over their mouths and stifled giggles.

"Give me that bag!" Koga shouted impatiently. He reached forward and grabbed the bag. Holding it upside down, Glam's uncle spilled the contents onto his desk. Out fell jelly beans, licorice sticks, Tum Tum's ninja suit, and more candy.

Koga looked up at Glam and narrowed his eyes into a fearsome squint.

"Uh-oh." Glam swallowed.

"Maybe it's in the suitcase," Slam said.

"I saw him put it in this bag," Glam insisted. "I swear, Uncle."

But his uncle didn't care.

"You have failed me again," Koga muttered. He snapped his fingers. "Ishikawa, demonstrate to my nephew how we handle fools."

91

The man in the white suit stepped toward Glam, who started to back up toward the tall windows forty-five stories above the streets of Tokyo.

"Uh, you know, Uncle, accidents do happen," Glam whimpered.

Without warning, Ishikawa picked up Glam, carried him over to the treadmill, and strapped his hands to its handlebars. Then the giant sumo wrestler turned on the treadmill to its highest speed.

Glam's legs flew out from under him. "Ahhhhh . . ." he screamed as the treadmill belt whipped around.

Ishikawa reached over and turned off the machine, causing the grunger's head to smack into the handlebars.

"Nephew," Koga said calmly. "I am much disappointed in you."

"Yeah, uh, sorry, Uncle," Glam replied in a whimper.

"But I am prepared to give you another chance," Koga said. "The old man, Mori Shintaro, he is in Tokyo?"

"Yes," Glam answered. "That's why we're here. We followed him."

Koga nodded. "Very well. Keep watching him. Listen to his every word. Find out where that dagger is and bring it to me."

"Yes!" Glam gasped. "Oh, yes, dearest uncle, my favorite relative."

Koga nodded at Ishikawa, who unstrapped Glam's hands and took him off the treadmill. Glam collapsed on the floor like a pool of warm Jell-O.

The grungers gave each other nervous looks. Slam kneeled down next to Glam. "Are you *sure* he's your favorite relative?" he whispered.

Glam just groaned.

Chapter 8

The boys were skateboarding on the street not far from their house. Tum Tum and Colt were crisscrossing each other's paths, and every time they did, Tum Tum would blow a bubble-gum bubble and Colt would reach out and try to pierce it with his hand.

Pop! He burst Tum Tum's bubble.

"Hey, Tum Tum," Colt said. "Now you owe me a piece."

"Here." Still riding his skateboard, Tum Tum reached into his pocket and tossed a piece of Bazooka to his brother.

"Hey, how about me?" Rocky asked.

"Oh, okay." Tum Tum tossed him a piece of gum, too.

Colt and Rocky stopped in the street to open their gum and read their fortunes. Tum Tum circled them on his skateboard. Colt read his fortune first.

"Listen to this, guys," he said, " 'Love will appear on a journey.' "

"You blew that one for us," Rocky said.

Colt looked up, slightly stung. "Hey, you voted to stay home, too."

"Yeah, I know." Rocky nodded regretfully. "But now I wish I hadn't."

"Besides," Tum Tum said as he circled them, "all love fortunes are for Rocky."

"That means you got mine," Colt said, pointing at the gum wrapper in Rocky's hand. "What's it say?"

Rocky held the fortune up close to his eyes and squinted at it.

"Well?" Tum Tum demanded.

"Uh . . ." Rocky squinted hard. "The letters are too tiny."

"So put on your glasses," Colt said. "Grandpa says you'll just make your eyes worse by squinting."

Rocky glanced questioningly at Tum Tum.

"Go ahead," Tum Tum said. "Put them on. I promise we won't make fun."

"Double promise?" Rocky asked.

"Double promise," Tum Tum replied.

Reluctantly Rocky took out his glasses. No sooner did he put them on than Tum Tum pretended to look scared.

"Ahh!" he shouted. "The four-eyed monster!"

Rocky glared at his little brother.

"So what's it say?" Colt asked.

Rocky looked down at the fortune. "It says, 'You have an insect for a brother. Squash him!' "

Without warning, Rocky lunged off his skateboard and tackled Tum Tum. The two of them went rolling onto a neighbor's lawn, wrestling playfully.

Behind him, Colt heard the sound of plastic wheels on asphalt, and turned to see three guys Rollerblading toward him. As they got closer, he felt a shiver of apprehension race down his spine. It was Keith, Darren, and Gerald, the guys from the Mustangs.

They rolled past Colt and up to the lawn where Tum Tum and Rocky were still wrestling.

"Hey, leave him alone," Keith said. "He's right."

Tum Tum and Rocky stopped wrestling.

"Yeah," said Darren with a nasty grin. "You *are* a four-eyed beast."

"And a lousy pitcher," Gerald added.

"Hey!" Tum Tum shouted, getting to his feet. "Only I can tell my brother that."

Rocky clenched his fists, but he knew he had to control himself. When the Mustangs players saw that they couldn't get a rise out of Rocky, they turned their attention elsewhere.

"And what do you call him?" Keith asked, pointing at Colt. "My Little Pony?" He turned to Colt and started making donkey noises again. "Hee-haw, hee-haw!"

Colt stepped off his skateboard and glared angrily at them. He felt as though he was just a fraction of an inch from beating Keith and the others into a pulp. But his grandfather's words echoed in his ears: *A ninja has self-control.*

Meanwhile, Keith was just asking for a fight. "Yeah, come on, Colt, do it," he taunted. "I'd love for you to try. Come on, make my day."

When Colt didn't respond, Keith stepped closer and gave him a shove. Colt raised his hands in assault position. He was just about ready to explode.

"Let's go, Colt," Rocky said.

But his brother didn't move. He just glared back at Keith.

"Colt, come on, let's go inside," Rocky said sternly. "Now, Colt."

Colt glared at his brother. "You're not my boss."

"I said *now*," Rocky yelled. When Colt still didn't move, Rocky grabbed him by the arm and pulled him away.

"Yeah, put him back in his stable!" Darren shouted with a laugh.

"See you on Sunday, Dra*goons!*" Gerald yelled, and his buddies laughed.

The three brothers got on their skateboards and headed home, with the taunting laughter of the Mustangs ringing in their ears.

A few moments later the boys went through the garage and into the kitchen of their house. Colt was peeved.

"Why'd you stop me, Rocky?" he asked. "You're acting like Grandpa."

Tum Tum pulled open one of the kitchen cabinets and took out a box of Mr. Chips cookies. "Yeah, Colt would've murderlized him."

"You made me look like a jerk in front of those guys," Colt moped.

The phone started to ring. As Rocky picked it up, the answering machine clicked on.

"Hello?" Rocky said. He heard a voice that sounded far away, but it was hard to tell who it was because the answering machine recording went on and Colt was still talking.

"Hey, Rocky, I was talking to you," Colt said.

"Colt, chill," Rocky snapped. "I think it's Grandpa."

"Grandpa!" Colt and Tum Tum cried at the same instant.

Halfway around the world, Grandpa Mori was sitting up in a hospital bed, wearing a hospital gown. He had a brace on his neck, and a small, stern-looking old nurse with a wrinkled face was slipping a blood-pressure cuff around his arm.

"How are you, Grandpa?" Rocky asked.

"I'm fine," Mori said. "But I'm in the hospital in Tokyo."

Rocky was on the kitchen phone. Colt

ran into the den and got on the phone there. Meanwhile, in the hospital room, the nurse tightened the blood-pressure cuff and started to pump it up.

"Ouch!" Mori yelped. "Not so hard!"

"What's wrong, Grandpa?" Colt asked.

"Yeah," said Rocky. "What happened?"

"Nothing, nothing, boys," Mori said. "I was in a tiny car accident."

"Were you hurt?" Colt asked, his voice etched with concern.

"No, no, just a few bruises," Grandpa Mori said. "But now I'm at the mercy of an ugly old witch posing as a nurse."

"Jeez, Grandpa," Rocky said. "Don't say that. She'll get mad at you."

"Don't worry, Rocky," Grandpa Mori replied. "This old bat doesn't understand a word of English."

The nurse, whose name was Hino, tightened the blood-pressure sleeve some more.

"*Ouch!*" Mori cried. "Leave me alone! I'm talking to my grandson."

"What's she doing to you?" Rocky asked.

"That's not important," Grandpa Mori replied. "What's important is that my bags got stolen."

"Even the bag with the dagger?" Rocky gasped.

"Yes, all of it. Even the bag with the dagger," Grandpa Mori said.

Tum Tum tapped Rocky on the shoulder. "What's he saying?"

"They stole the dagger," Rocky whispered.

"Uh-oh!" Tum Tum gasped.

In the hospital room, Nurse Hino began to unwrap the blood pressure cuff from around Mori's arm.

"Ouch!" Mori shouted at her. "Take it easy, you vampire."

Nurse Hino made a face at him.

"Grandpa," Rocky said over the phone. "What did the guys who stole it look like?"

"There were three guys," Mori said. "One was a weird-looking Asian guy with long white hair. The other two were just creeps."

"Did you tell the police?" Rocky asked.

"Forget about them," Grandpa Mori said. "Just don't tell your parents about this. I don't want them to worry. I just wanted you to know."

"I promise we won't tell anyone," Rocky said.

"You sure they're taking good care of you?" Colt asked, still concerned.

"Yes, yes, Colt," Mori said. "I'm in Tokyo General. It's a fine hospital, except for this wicked nurse."

At that, the nurse, gave the blood pressure cuff a final yank.

Rippp!

"*Yeow!*" Grandpa Mori screeched.

Nurse Hino smiled maliciously. "You will be surprised to know that some people around here *do* understand English, Mr. Shintaro."

Grandpa Mori stared at her with wide, astonished eyes. Then he turned back to the phone. "Uh, I think I better go, boys."

"Okay, Grandpa," Rocky said. "I hope you feel better. Bye."

They hung up. Tokyo General Hospital, Rocky reminded himself. Colt came back into the kitchen from the den. Tum Tum started going through the kitchen cabinets.

"Anyone see my fat-free Ding Dongs?" he asked.

Colt and Rocky ignored him.

"I missed the part where Grandpa said who stole the dagger," Colt said.

"He said it was some Asian guy with white hair," Rocky answered.

"Like that jerko metalhead at the cabin?" Tum Tum asked.

Rocky's jaw dropped. He looked at Colt, who stared back, equally amazed.

"Oh, no!" Rocky gasped.

"Those guys are in Japan with Grandpa!" Colt said.

Meanwhile, Tum Tum had finished searching the kitchen cabinets. Now he turned to his ninja bag and opened it.

"Huh?" Tum Tum frowned.

"What now?" Rocky asked.

"This isn't my bag," Tum Tum said, reaching into it. "It's Grandpa's. And look!"

Tum Tum took out the dagger.

"Oh, wow," Rocky said. "Grandpa's really in trouble now. Those guys are after the dagger, and when they figure out that it wasn't in his luggage, they're gonna go after him again."

"We gotta go there right away," Colt said. "We gotta help him."

103

"But what about the game on Sunday, Colt?" Rocky asked.

"It's just a game," Colt said. "This is Grandpa, and he needs us. Blood is thicker than soda."

"You realize those guys not only got my bag?" Tum Tum asked. "They got my Ding Dongs, too."

"Forget the Ding Dongs, Tum Tum," Rocky said. "We've got a lot to do. First we have to get airplane tickets."

"How?" Colt asked.

Rocky took Mori's bag and dumped it out on the kitchen table. A gold credit card fell out, and Rocky picked it up.

"You're gonna use that?" Colt asked nervously.

"Grandpa would want us to," Rocky said.

"But how're you gonna do it?" Tum Tum asked. "If you go to the travel agency, they'll see you're not Grandpa."

That was a problem. But Rocky had an idea.

"I know!" he said. "We'll call the airline directly, like Dad does."

"Even if they can't see you, you still sound like a kid," Colt said.

Rocky knew his brother had a good point. Still, there had to be a way. One of the cardinal ninja rules was to use everything around you. Rocky looked around. He noticed that the red light on the answering machine on the kitchen counter was blinking. Of course! The answering machine had recorded the conversation he'd just had with Grandpa!

"Okay, here's what we'll do," Rocky said, huddling with his brothers.

A few minutes later, Rocky dialed the number of Air Japan. A ticket agent answered and Rocky told her he needed three tickets on the next flight to Japan for him and his brothers.

"Children's fares?" the ticket agent asked.

"Well, we're almost grown-up," Rocky said.

"And how will you pay?"

"Uh, credit card."

"I see." The ticket agent sounded a little suspicious. "And the name on the credit card?"

"Mori Shintaro," Rocky said. "He's my grandfather."

"I'm afraid we'll need his authorization," the ticket agent said. "Can I speak to him?"

"Uh, sure," Rocky said, and winked at Colt. Rocky put the phone next to the answering machine, and Colt started to replay parts of the conversation they'd just had with their grandfather.

"Hello?" Mori said on the tape.

"Mr. Shintaro?" said the ticket agent. "How are you today?"

Colt quickly pressed REWIND, then PLAY at the point where Grandpa Mori said, "I'm fine."

"That's nice," said the ticket agent. "I just took a reservation on your card from a young man."

"My grandson," Mori said from the tape.

"Yes," said the ticket agent. "That's what he told me. Three seats on this afternoon's flight to — "

"Tokyo," Mori said.

"So I have your authorization?" the ticket agent asked.

Colt accidentally hit the PLAY button a little too soon, and they heard their grandfather say, "Ouch! Not so hard!"

Rocky made a face at Colt, who mouthed the word *Sorry*.

"I beg your pardon," said the confused ticket agent. "Is this amount okay with you?"

"Yes, all of it," Mori replied. Before Colt could stop it, the tape jumped, and they heard their grandfather say, "You vampire!"

"Well, really, sir, I don't set the prices," said the ticket agent. "I just work the phones. I'll run this through the computer. Your grandsons can pick up the tickets at the airport." Then she added, "And have a nice day," although it was clear she didn't mean it.

Colt moved the tape to the point where he thought Mori said good-bye, but instead his grandfather said, "Ugly old witch."

"Oh, yeah?" the ticket agent snapped irately. "Well, you know what *you* are? You're a — "

Rocky quickly cut her short, shouting "Good-bye!" into the phone and hanging up. He turned to Colt and Tum Tum. "Okay, we really gotta get it in gear. I'll write a note to Mom and Dad. Colt, you find all the money in the house. Tum Tum, you call a cab. We'll be packed when it gets here."

"How're we gonna do all that before Mom and Dad get home?" Tum Tum asked.

"You've heard of ingenuity?" Rocky replied. "Well, this is ninja-nuity. Now go!"

The three boys raced through the house, preparing for their trip. Fifteen minutes later they were just about ready to go when the doorbell rang.

"Oh, no," Rocky gasped. "Mom and Dad?"

Colt peeked out the living room window. "It's the taxi!"

"Come on, we gotta go!" Rocky yelled.

Tum Tum came out of his room and went halfway down the stairs, then stopped. "I don't want to leave Mom and Dad," he sniffed.

"What are you talking about?" Rocky asked. "You were the one who wanted to go to Japan in the first place."

"But that was with Grandpa," Tum Tum replied.

"Well, we'll see him when we get there," Colt said.

But Tum Tum wouldn't budge. Rocky thought he understood what the problem was. Going to Japan sounded great to Tum Tum when it was just a word and an idea, but now that they were really going halfway around the world, he felt a little nervous.

"Look, Tum Tum," he said, "I promise everything will be okay. We're going for Grandpa, remember? And I hear the Japanese have really good candy."

Tum Tum studied him suspiciously. "Are you making that up?"

"No way," Rocky said, although he was. "Now come on, we really have to go or we're going to miss the plane."

Tum Tum sighed and came down the stairs. As he went through the entryway, he saw a photograph of his mom and dad. He picked it up and put it in his bag.

Moments later the boys were sitting in the back of the cab as it sped to the airport. The cab screeched to a halt at the curb, and the boys jumped and raced through the terminal. Ahead at the Air Japan gate, a flight attendant was just about to close the door.

"Wait!" Rocky cried.

The flight attendant looked up surprised as the three boys hustled past her, thumped down the walkway, and into the jet.

Moments later the jumbo jet backed out of the gate and taxied down the runway for takeoff. In their seats, each of the boys was lost in his own thoughts. Rocky wondered if they'd done the right thing by running off to Japan. Colt wondered if Grandpa Mori was still okay. Tum Tum wondered where the lady with the soda and peanuts was . . .

"Boys?" Jessica Douglas called as she walked into the dark house after work and flicked on the lights. "Boys, where are you?"

A chill of apprehension rushed through her. The boys should have been home. Her house shouldn't have been dark and quiet. It should have been ablaze with lights and filled with noise.

Then she noticed the note and instantly felt relieved. They'd gone somewhere and left a note. Jessica was pleased. She was always nagging them about leaving a note if they were going somewhere, and she was glad that they'd obeyed. She picked up the note and scanned it:

Dear Mom and Dad,
   We've gone to Japan. Be back
soon.
                 Rocky, Colt, and Tum Tum

"*AHHHHHHHHHHHHH!*" Jessica's
scream tore out of her throat and echoed
through the empty house.

Chapter 9

Many hours later the boys stood on the curb in front of the main terminal at Tokyo Airport. The scene was almost overwhelming. Dozens of cars and hundreds of people were rushing to and from the curb. Loudspeakers barked announcements in Japanese.

"Wow," Colt gasped as the boys huddled close together.

"Rocky?" Tum Tum looked up at his big brother nervously.

Rocky put his hand on Tum Tum's shoulder. "It's cool, Tum Tum. We'll just stick together. We'll get a cab to Tokyo General Hospital."

"YIEEE!" A scream cut through the din.

The boys looked up and saw a mugger in dark clothes accosting an elderly woman in a green kimono near a limousine. The mugger was trying to grab her handbag and the old woman was shrieking and hitting him with her free hand.

The mugger was stronger than the woman and soon pulled the bag out of her grasp and started to push away through the crowd.

"What can we do?" Tum Tum asked.

"We're too far away to grab him," Rocky said, frustrated.

Colt had an idea. He opened his ninja bag and tossed Rocky a baseball. "Beanball, Rocky."

Rocky grinned, wound up, and delivered a perfect strike.

Thunk! The ball conked the mugger squarely in the back of the head, knocking him to the ground. The handbag went flying.

"Nice pitch," Colt said. "What was it, a fastball?"

"Split-finger," Rocky said with a nod.

The mugger staggered to his feet and ran

away. Tum Tum ran over to the spot where he'd fallen and picked up the purse. When he handed it back to the old woman, she nodded many times and said a bunch of stuff in Japanese.

Now a chauffeur in a gray uniform hurried over. He and the old woman had a fast conversation, then the chauffeur turned to the boys.

"She thanks you very much," he said, translating for her. "She wants to repay you."

The boys looked at each other. Then Rocky said, "Could you give us a ride to Tokyo General Hospital?"

The chauffeur talked to the old woman. Then he turned back to the boys. "She wants to know, are you sick?"

"No, we're fine," Rocky explained. "But our grandfather's in the hospital and we came to see him."

"His name's Mori Shintaro," Tum Tum said. "Do you know him?"

"No," said the chauffeur, opening the door for them, "but it will be our pleasure to take you to him."

The boys got into the limo and looked around with grins on their faces.

"Wow, this is really loaded!" Colt whispered. "TV, CD player, small refrigerator, the works!"

The old woman smiled at them as if she knew what Colt was saying. She opened the small refrigerator and then said something to the chauffeur, who'd gotten into the front and started to drive.

"She asked if you'd like something to eat?" he said.

"Well, if you insist," Tum Tum replied. "What is it?"

"*Sashimi*," said the chauffeur. "Raw fish."

The woman took a plate out of the refrigerator and handed it to Tum Tum, along with a pair of chopsticks. On it were thick white and pink slabs of fish. Colt and Rocky made disgusted faces, but Tum Tum just shrugged.

"Hey, guys," he said, "when in Rome . . ." Then he started to scarf the fish down.

The boys had so much fun riding in the limo and looking at the sights that they were almost sorry when they got to Tokyo General Hospital. They thanked the old lady and the chauffeur and went inside.

Thanks to an English-speaking person at the information desk, they found out that their grandfather was on the third floor.

The boys took the elevator up and started down the hall on the third floor, past rooms with ill people lying in beds. Fortunately, the room numbers were the same in Japanese and English.

"Three-oh-one," Rocky read the number above a door. "Three-oh-two . . . It should be down at the end of this hall."

"*Arrrgghhhh!*" A cry reached their ears. The boys looked startled.

"That sounded like Grandpa!" Colt gasped.

"Sounds like he's in trouble!" said Rocky.

The boys rushed the rest of the way down the hall and into their grandfather's room. Grandpa Mori was lying on his stomach. An old woman in a white uniform was pulling the bedclothes over him. In one hand she held an empty syringe.

"Gross," Tum Tum groaned when he saw the needle.

"Can't you be a little bit more gentle, Nurse Hino?" Mori asked.

"Really, Mr. Shintaro," Nurse Hino replied. "My grandchildren behave better than you."

"Well, *my* grandchildren would drive you out of town with a ninja stick for what you did," Mori shot back.

"He's right," Tum Tum said. "We would."

"See?" Grandpa Mori said. "You tell her, Tum Tum." Then Mori did a double-take. "Tum Tum! Boys! What are you doing here?"

Mori rose up on his elbows and the boys rushed to him. He hugged them joyfully.

"There's something really important we have to tell you," Rocky said.

Mori looked over at Colt. "But what about the baseball game?"

Colt just shrugged sheepishly. Grandpa Mori smiled.

"Well, I'm very glad to see you," he said and turned to the nurse. "Nurse Hino, these are my three ninjas." He pointed at the syringe. "Now take that away. Come back later."

Nurse Hino left. Grandpa Mori turned back to the boys. "Now tell me what's so important," he said.

"We think you're in a lot of danger, Grandpa," Colt said.

"Danger?" Mori scowled. "What danger?"

On the street in front of Tokyo General Hospital, Slam and Vinnie sat in a hi-tech surveillance van that Koga had rented for them. From the outside, the van looked very ordinary, but inside it was chockful of recording decks, microphones, and video equipment. Vinnie sat at the electronic controls while Slam unrolled some posters he'd just purchased.

"Man, this is state-of-the-art digital equipment," Vinnie said enthusiastically. "We could record some major tunes on this machinery, don't you think, Slam?"

Just then sounds began to crackle out of one of the speakers above him.

"Testing one, two, three, dudes," Glam's voice echoed through the van. "I'm almost at the old dude's room."

On the third floor of the hospital, Glam, dressed as an orderly in green surgical scrubs, mask, and cap, pushed a pill cart into Mori's room. His long platinum hair was tucked up under the cap. Mori and the boys hardly noticed him.

"You know the guy you said stole your luggage?" Rocky was saying. "The Japanese guy with the long white hair?"

"Yes?" Mori said.

"He's the same guy who tried to rob the cabin," Colt said.

Glam tried not to react as he opened a pill jar and took out a small microphone.

"How do you know that?" Mori asked.

"Did he look like a heavy-metal chump?" Rocky asked.

"Like he was trying to be a grunge rock stud?" asked Colt.

"But just came off like a major drip instead?" added Rocky.

"Well . . ." Mori thought for a moment. "Yes, that was him exactly."

Glam winced, and proceeded to plant the bugging device near the bed. Then he went back to the pill cart and pushed it out of the room.

Down in the surveillance van, Vinnie could now hear Mori and the boys' conversation cleary. Meanwhile, Slam had put on a pair of headphones and was lurching around the van, playing air guitar.

"There were three of them," Mori said

over the speaker. "I really didn't get a good look at the other two. Just the one with the fake-looking hair."

"He's right!" Vinnie muttered. "It does look fake."

Just at that moment, Glam yanked open the van's door and climbed in front, still wearing the orderly's uniform and cap. He angled the rearview mirror toward himself and pulled off the surgical cap. Underneath it, his long platinum hair was squashed into a cylinder.

"Emergency!" Glam shouted and started fluffing out his hair. "Hat hair! Hat hair!"

"Shut up!" Vinnie snapped. "I'm trying to listen."

Over the speakers they heard Colt say that he thought the three grungers were after the dagger.

"Well, they have my bag, so they have it now," Mori replied.

"No, they don't," Rocky said. "We have it."

"Rocky, how?" Mori asked.

"You took Tum Tum's bag by mistake," Rocky said.

"And they got my Ding Dongs," Tum Tum said.

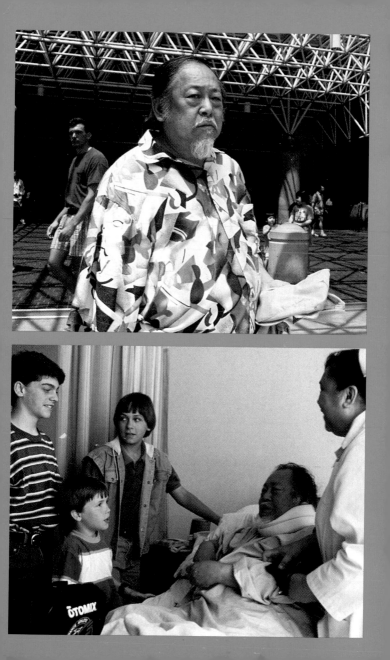

"You hear that?" Vinnie asked. "Those kids have the dagger!"

"All right!" Glam said as he finished fluffing out his hair.

"What's all right about it?" Slam asked, pulling off his headphones.

"If they got it, we can get it," Glam said.

"Hey, quiet," Vinnie hushed them. "They're talking again."

The grungers quieted down and listened.

"So you came all this way because you thought I was in trouble?" Grandpa Mori asked. He sounded proud of them. "What did you tell your parents?"

"Well, uh, we . . ." Rocky stammered guiltily.

Up in the room, Grandpa Mori shook his head and groaned. "Oh, no . . ."

"We did leave them a note," Colt said hopefully.

Mori reached for the phone beside his bed and started to punch in numbers. "You must talk to them," he said as he dialed. "In the meantime, we must make plans for the dagger."

Halfway around the world Jessica answered the phone.

"Hello, Jessica," Mori said. "It's Dad. How

are you? How's the weather over there?"

Even across the room the boys could hear their mother's shrill voice over the phone.

"The boys?" Mori pretended to play dumb. "Oh, let me see. Yes, they *are* here. Yes, yes, hold on a second."

Grandpa Mori put his hand over the receiver and held the phone out toward the boys. "She's angry," he whispered.

The boys backed away from the phone, shaking their heads.

"Come on," Mori whispered. "Take the phone. You're not scared, are you?"

The boys nodded in unison.

"Then just let her know you're alive," Mori whispered, taking his hand off the receiver.

"*Hello, Mom!*" the boys called together. They signaled for their grandfather to talk to her. Mori gave them a disappointed shake of his head and then brought the phone back to his ear.

"Now, now, honey," he said, trying to mollify his irate daughter. "It's not their fault. I told them to come. Why? Because I missed them."

The boys couldn't hear their mother's voice anymore. Grandpa Mori winked at them, letting them know that she'd calmed down.

"Yes, yes," he said into the phone. "I'll take good care of them. They'll be fine. Here, talk to Tum Tum."

Now that he knew his mom had calmed down, Tum Tum was eager to take the phone.

"Hi, Mom," he said brightly. "The trip was cool. Yeah, we're all fine. Guess what? I ate raw fish!"

While Tum Tum talked to Jessica, Grandpa Mori turned to Rocky and Colt and started to write something on a piece of paper. "The tournament is going on in Konang right now," he said. "I can't leave the hospital yet, so you boys must take the dagger there for me. You can present it to the winner of the competition."

Meanwhile, Tum Tum was frowning as he talked on the phone. "What? Oh, Mom, come on."

The boys' mother started to get loud again. Tum Tum held the phone away from his ear, and they all listened.

"You will do this for me," Jessica said sternly. "Set the beeper on your watch and call us every day at seven A.M. Tokyo time. Got that? No arguing. You're still not out of trouble. For Pete's sake, leaving me a note like you were just going to the store or something."

Tum Tum brought the phone back to his ear. "Okay, Mom, okay. Seven A.M. every morning. I got it." He set his watch and held out the phone to the other boys. "Mom wants to say good-bye."

"Bye, Mom," Colt and Rocky yelled together. Tum Tum hung up the phone.

"She say anything about Dad?" Colt asked nervously.

"He's away on a business trip," Tum Tum reported. "She says he'll have plenty to say when he gets back."

Colt glanced at Rocky, who bit his lip and shrugged. All three boys turned back to their grandfather.

"But what about you, Grandpa?" Colt asked.

"They say they'll let me go in two days," Mori said. "As soon as I get out of this jail, I'll come straight to Konang and join you."

Just then Nurse Hino came back into the room with another syringe and a wicked smile on her face.

"Not you again," Mori said. "Didn't I tell you to go away?"

"Do you know how I deal with trouble-some patients?" Nurse Hino smiled sweetly, but a moment later her smile disappeared. She stepped close to a wooden dresser.

"*Hi-yah!*" she screamed as her hand sliced down through the air.

Crash! The top of the dresser shattered under the blow. The boys jumped back, and even Mori looked frightened.

"Now roll over!" Nurse Hino barked, stepping toward the bed with the syringe ready.

"Wait, wait!" Grandpa Mori gasped. "I'll make a deal with you. You can use me as a pincushion if you agree to help me."

"How?" Nurse Hino asked.

"See to it that my boys get on the train to Konang," Mori said.

"That's okay, Grandpa," Rocky said. "We can get there ourselves."

"Tokyo's a big city, boys," Mori warned

them. "Even ninjas need help now and then."

"I'll be glad to help them if it means you'll behave," Nurse Hino said. "I have grand-children of my own. And anyway, this is the end of my shift."

"Thank God," Mori muttered.

"Nurse Shabuya will be taking my place," Nurse Hino added.

Another nurse came into the room. She was bigger, uglier, and meaner-looking than Nurse Hino. Nurse Hino handed her the syringe, and Nurse Shabuya headed toward Mori with a menacing smile on her lips.

"Come, boys," Nurse Hino said, herding the boys out of the room. "Your grand-father wants to be alone now."

The boys stepped out into the hall.

"No! No! *Ahhhhhhh!*" Grandpa Mori screamed behind them.

Chapter 10

A little while later the boys left the hospital, carrying their bags in single file with Nurse Hino marching behind them like a drill sergeant.

"Dudes!" Glam pointed through the windshield of the van. "There they go! And there goes the bag with the dagger!"

"Time to follow on foot," Vinnie said, pushing open the van's door. The grungers jumped out and followed Nurse Hino and the boys to a nearby fish market, where Nurse Hino bought some squid for dinner. Next they stopped in a sporting-goods store, where the boys looked over the Jap-

anese baseball equipment while Nurse
Hino tried out the weights.

The grungers almost got their chance to
grab Tum Tum's bag in an incredibly noisy
pachinko parlor, where the boys were distracted by the flashing lights and rattling
pachinko games. They were similar to pin-
ball machines, except they hung vertically
on the wall and used dozens of small silver
balls. Tum Tum had just bought a new plastic bag of *pachinko* balls and was heading
back to his machine when Vinnie snuck up
behind him. He was just about to grab Tum
Tum's ninja bag when the plastic bag suddenly broke and a hundred little *pachinko*
balls flooded over the floor.

"*Ahhhhhhh!*" Vinnie slipped and flipped
into the air.

"*Ooof!*" *Bonk! Thud!* Slam and Glam ran
over to catch him, and the three fell into a
heap.

Just then, Nurse Hino waved to the
boys. "Boys, your train is leaving!"

Tum Tum and Rocky grabbed their bags
and hurried out of the parlor, but Colt sat
at the game, transfixed.

"Are you coming, young man?" Nurse
Hino asked.

"In a second," Colt replied.

But Nurse Hino wasn't interested in waiting. She marched over to the boy, grabbed him by the ear, and twisted.

"Yeow!" Colt cried. He grabbed his bag and quickly followed.

They followed Nurse Hino to the train station, and were followed in turn by the grungers.

"Whoa, dudes!" Glam gasped, pointing at the train platform. "They're getting on the train!"

"This is our last chance to get the dagger!" Vinnie cried.

"Kamikaze mission!" Slam yelled.

The three grungers charged toward the boys, but at the last second Nurse Hino stepped in their way.

"Unh!"

"Ooof"

"Huh!"

The grungers smacked into her and bounced back as if they'd run into a solid brick wall.

"Get out of the way, you old bag," Glam yelled.

Nurse Hino's eyes narrowed, and she got into a karate stance.

"Give us a break," Vinnie said, rolling his eyes at the little old nurse.

"Yeah," said Slam with a smirk. "I mean, you don't really think you can take all three of us, do you?"

"*Aiiiiiiieeeeee!*" Nurse Hino answered with a shriek, and she leaped into the air.

Wham! Pow! Boink! The next thing the grungers knew, they were lying on their backs on the train platform, and the train was pulling away.

Later that day the boys arrived in Konang, a rural town about fifty miles north of Tokyo. Unlike Tokyo's massive urban center and tall buildings, Konang featured homes made of bamboo, low wooden buildings, and beautiful red-and-green Buddhist temples. The boys took a cab from the train station to the Konang *dojo* where the karate tournament was in progress. The *dojo* was a large building with a silver tile roof and ornately designed wooden doors.

"Wow, cool place," Colt said.

"Yeah, this is a lot more the way I imagined Japan would look," agreed Rocky.

They were just about to go in when Tum

Tum spotted two huge sumo wrestlers walking by. Both were wearing long white robes, and their black hair was pulled up on their heads in sumo knots.

Maybe they're going somewhere to eat, Tum Tum thought, and started to follow them, but his brothers grabbed him and led him into the *dojo*.

No sooner had the boys passed through the large wooden doors than they became aware of cheering and shouting and other crowd noises. As they walked down a dimly lit hall lined with framed photographs of ninja masters, the sounds grew louder.

"Oh, wow, look!" Colt gasped. They'd come to a large courtyard area in the center of the *dojo*. It was surrounded on three sides by bleachers filled with yelling, cheering fans. On the fourth side sat rows of young fighters, wearing brightly colored team uniforms, patiently waiting their turns to do battle in the center of the room, which was covered with a huge orange mat. On the mat, several boys in bright yellow costumes were stretching and warming up.

The people in the stands kept yelling and cheering in Japanese. Many of the men held video cameras. Down near the mats, an angry mother stood in front of the official's table, arguing with a referee wearing a black-and-white striped shirt.

"Amazing," Rocky said. "It's just like our baseball team."

"Hey!" Colt suddenly said, looking around. "Where's Tum Tum?"

Tum Tum had disappeared. His older brothers started to look around. Then Rocky noticed a smell in the air.

"You smell that?" he asked Colt.

Colt nodded. "Smells like roasted chicken."

Rocky spotted a vendor nearby. The smell was coming from his cart.

"Wouldn't you know it," Colt said with an amused look. Tum Tum was standing in line behind several other hungry customers, waiting for the vendor to sell them something that looked like chunks of chicken on a stick.

"If we went to the North Pole, that kid would find the Eskimo Pie vendor," Rocky said with a laugh.

Tum Tum bought his treat and returned to his brothers.

"You are amazing," Colt said, shaking his head.

"What is it, anyway?" Rocky asked.

"Chicken *yakitori*," Tum Tum said through a mouthful of chicken. "It's good. You should get one."

"Uh, maybe later," Rocky said. "Let's sit."

As the boys took seats, the crowd began to quiet down. Colt sat between Rocky and Tum Tum. An impressive-looking older man wearing a magnificent white robe with red flowers and blue butterflies printed on it stepped onto the mat. He wore a white-and-blue mask with a long white beard hanging from the chin.

"Who's that?" Tum Tum asked.

"Bet it's the grand master," Colt said.

The grand master beckoned to two young contestants. One wore white, and the other, crimson. Both uniforms covered much of their faces. One wore a number 7 on his back. The other wore 12. The grand master spoke to them briefly and then backed off the mat. The two contestants bowed and took up karate stances.

"The games begin," Colt whispered.

"Heeee-yaahhhh!" Number 7 let out a soul-piercing scream and the fight began.

"Wow!" Tum Tum put his hands over his ears. "I never heard anyone scream like that. Is this what Grandpa wants us to learn? The next level of screaming?"

"Grow up," Colt muttered.

The contest was over almost before it began. Number 7 was declared the winner.

"Jeez, he's really good," Rocky said.

"I could take him," Colt said with a shrug.

"You'll never know," Rocky said.

Colt bit his lip. He was just itching to get out there.

The tournament progressed as other contestants faced each other and fought.

"Hey, look." A little while later Tum Tum pointed toward the contestants waiting their turn. "It's number 7's turn again."

Once again, number 7 let out a shrill scream and demolished his opponent easily. Colt leaned forward in his seat, studying every move. He wished he could get out there.

"The kid is *dangerous*," Rocky said reverently.

Colt just wanted his chance. As the tournament continued, he noticed that number 16 had twisted his ankle and was sitting on the sidelines with an ice pack on his foot. His parents hovered around him with consoling expressions on their faces, but the kid looked really upset. It was obvious he was too badly hurt to continue.

Colt glanced over at a tall board behind the official's table. It showed two rows of numbers. Suddenly he realized that it was indicating who each competitor would face next. Next to number 16 was . . . number 7!

Meanwhile, down below, number 16's parents were helping him out of his bright yellow uniform. Colt watched as they held his arms and he hobbled away, leaving the robe and mask behind.

The temptation was too great.

"I'll be right back," Colt said, getting up.

"Where're you going?" Tum Tum asked.

"I just want to take a look around." With that, Colt vanished into the crowd.

A little while later, number 7 returned to the mat for his next match. An official rose from the official's table and began to remove the sixteen from the board behind the table.

Just then number 16 hurried onto the mat.

The officials looked puzzled. Some whispers and headshaking followed, but the official rose again and put 16 back on the board.

The two contestants faced each other and bowed.

"Hee-yahhh!" Number 7 launched his attack with the now familiar high-pitched scream. Number 16 fought back valiantly.

"Looks like number 7's finally found some competition," Rocky said.

"Yeah, number 16's not bad," Tum Tum said.

Down on the mat, the fight progressed.

"He's kind of wild, though," Rocky said. "Like Colt."

"That's what I was thinking," Tum Tum said, "He really reminds me of . . ."

The realization hit Rocky and Tum Tum at the same time. They stared at each other across the empty space where their brother had been sitting.

"Colt!" they gasped at the same time.

Tum Tum jumped up. "Come on, he's gonna get his brains splattered."

But Rocky grabbed his brother's shoulder and pulled him back down. "Let him fight," he said. "Remember Grandpa said he needed to learn a lesson?"

"Yeah?"

"Well, maybe this is it."

Colt put up a good fight, but he was no match for the superior skills of number 7. Finally Colt went down. The crowd applauded appreciatively, and number 7 pulled off his mask.

Even from up in the stands, Tum Tum and Rocky could see the shocked expression on their brother's face.

Number 7 was a girl.

"A girl?" Tum Tum gasped in bewildered disgust.

Next to him, Rocky slipped on his glasses for a better look. She had long black hair and a beautiful, soft face. Despite the ferociousness with which she fought, she had small, delicate features. "A girl," he whispered with an intrigued smile.

The crowd continued to clap, and the grand master started out onto the mat.

"I get the feeling it's over," Rocky said. "Looks like miss number 7 won."

"If she's the winner, does that mean we give her the dagger?" Tum Tum asked.

"We better go ask Mr. Big," Rocky said, gesturing to the grand master.

The boys headed down to the mats. Meanwhile, number 7 stepped over to Colt and offered her hand to help him up. Tum Tum and Rocky joined Colt. Number 7 had turned away to talk to the grand master.

"Good fight," Rocky said, patting Colt on his back.

"Not good enough," Colt replied.

Meanwhile, Tum Tum had become fascinated by the grand master's large, callused bare feet.

"Wow, look at those feet!" he gasped. "I think he's Fred Flintstone."

Colt nudged him with his elbow. "Even in Japan you're a doofus."

"Maybe," Tum Tum shot back, "but at least I didn't get beaten by a girl!"

Rocky approached the grand master. Back home, he'd been studying Japanese with Grandpa Mori and had learned a few phrases, but as soon as he started to talk, the grand master replied with a torrent of Japanese Rocky couldn't follow.

"I'm sorry," Rocky stammered. "You're going too fast."

"Perhaps I can help," said the girl. "I speak some English."

"Great," Rocky said. "Could you tell him we have this dagger from our grandfather, Mori Shintaro?"

As the girl translated, Rocky pulled the dagger out of his grandfather's ninja bag. Suddenly the crowd in the stands hushed.

"Wow," Colt whispered to Tum Tum. "I guess they all know what it is."

But Tum Tum still couldn't take his eyes off the grand master's feet.

"What do you want to bet he's ticklish?" he whispered back, bending down and sticking out his finger to tickle the grand master's feet.

"Are you crazy?" Colt hissed, grabbing his little brother and pulling him back.

The grand master spoke to the girl, who then turned toward Rocky. "He says he knew you were coming. Your grandfather called from Tokyo. He says he's sorry your grandfather is hurt and he hopes he gets better."

"Tell him thanks," Rocky said.

The girl translated, and the grand master nodded and spoke again.

"He says the ceremony will wait two days until Mori Shintaro arrives," the girl said. "He says it is important to uphold tradition."

"What should we do with the dagger till then?" Tum Tum asked.

"I will take it," the girl offered. She reached eagerly for the dagger, but the grand master stopped her and spoke in Japanese. The girl looked disappointed and turned to Rocky.

"The grand master says if your grandfather trusted you with the dagger, so does he," she explained.

The grand master bowed to the boys and turned away.

"Uh, what should we do now?" Tum Tum asked.

"You come with me," said the girl. She led them toward the sideline, where an older woman waited. From their similar looks, and the proud, beaming expression on the woman's face, Rocky deduced that she was the girl's mother.

Meanwhile, Tum Tum kept ribbing Colt. "Colt got beat by a girl. . . . Colt got beat by a girl," he chanted in a whisper.

"I'm still better than *you*," Colt snapped.

"Shut up, spaz," Tum Tum shot back.

The girl turned back to Colt. "You are a worthy opponent, Spaz."

Tum Tum and Rocky both chuckled, and Colt's face turned red.

"No, the name's Colt," he explained. "And this is Rocky and Tum Tum."

"I am Miyo Shikigawa," the girl said. "This my mother."

The boys bowed to her and Miyo's mother bowed back.

"I would love to hear about America," Miyo said. "Do you live near Bart Simpson?"

"Right around the corner," Tum Tum said.

"Really?" Miyo looked excited.

"No, he's kidding you," Rocky said.

Miyo looked a little disappointed. "Where are you staying in Konang?" she asked.

The boys glanced at each other and shrugged.

"We don't know," Colt said.

"We really didn't plan anything," added Rocky.

"Then you will come home with us!" Miyo said.

"You sure?" Rocky asked.

Miyo nodded and spoke rapidly in Japanese to her mother, who also nodded. Now Mrs. Shikigawa turned to the boys.

"We would be honored," she said. "But first, we must hurry. We have one important place to go."

The boys gave each other puzzled looks and followed Miyo and her mother out to their car. They all got in, and Mrs. Shikigawa drove them through the town, parking next to a broad, flat field with a tall wire backstop.

"A baseball field!" Colt cried.

Other cars were pulling up, and kids with mitts and bats were getting out and running over to the field.

"Wow, what is this?" Tum Tum asked. "A game?"

"No," Miyo replied. "It is . . ." She frowned. "How do you say it? Many people want few positions?"

"A tryout!" Rocky said.

142

Miyo nodded and smiled. "Yes, a tryout. If I am good, I am on the team."

"Well, cool," Colt said, pushing open the car door. "Let's go."

The boys got out of the car. Almost immediately they smelled the scent of roasted chicken. Tum Tum spun around and spotted another *yakitori* cart.

"Be right back," he said, and took off.

Miyo watched him and laughed.

"Your brother," she said to Colt and Rocky. "He is hungry?"

"All the time," Rocky and Colt replied with exaggerated nods.

Miyo's mom got her daughter's mitt out of the car trunk and handed it to her.

"I will go to try out now," Miyo told the boys. "You will not mind waiting?"

"Naw, it's cool," said Colt.

"Yeah, and good luck," said Rocky.

Miyo blushed slightly. "Thank you," she said. "I will need it."

Miyo headed out to the field while the boys and her mother stood on the sidelines with the other spectators. A man who looked like a coach told Miyo to get a bat.

"Looks like she's gonna hit," Tum Tum said, holding a *yakitori* stick.

A kid on the pitcher's mound threw the ball, and Miyo took a swing.

Clack! She hit a short pop-up. Five kids rushed forward to catch it.

"Wow, she's got a lot of competition," Rocky said.

On the next pitch, Miyo hit a grounder. On the next, she hit a line drive. Rocky looked over at the coach. The man nodded.

"I think he's impressed," he whispered.

Miyo's mother nodded, but didn't appear encouraged.

"Every year she is the only girl to try out," she said with a sigh.

"Don't worry," Colt said, trying to make her feel better. "She hit pretty well. I bet if she tries really hard, she'll make it."

"Every year she tries really hard," Mrs. Shikigawa replied. "But there are many others who also try hard."

Tum Tum looked across the field. On a hill overlooking the town, he spotted a sturdy-looking stone castle. Its walls were white and its roof was blue tile.

"What's that?" he asked, pointing his *yakitori* stick.

"Castle Hikone," Miyo's mother answered.

"Who lives there?" Tum Tum asked. "The evil umpire?"

Colt nudged him in the ribs with his elbow. "You mean emperor, lamebrain."

"No, I mean umpire," Tum Tum said.

Miyo's mother shook her head. "No one lives there," she said. "It is very, very old."

"Wow," said Rocky. "I'm surprised they haven't turned it into condos."

Out on the field, the coach yelled something to Miyo, who quickly put down her bat and picked up her glove.

"Here is the real test," Mrs. Shikigawa said softly to the boys.

Miyo got into short centerfield and turned around.

"There must be twenty kids out there!" Tum Tum gasped.

Crack! A new kid at the plate hit a high pop-up. A bunch of kids ran toward it, but Miyo got there first.

Plop! The ball hit Miyo's mitt and fell out. Another kid quickly picked it up and threw it to the pitcher. Miyo watched with sagging shoulders.

"Maybe she better stick to ninja," Colt mumbled.

"Shut up." Rocky gave him a shove.

A few minutes later another batter hit a hard grounder at Miyo. She bent down to get it, but it rolled right through her legs. The coach shook his head and started toward her.

"Uh-oh," Tum Tum whispered.

They watched as the coach spoke to Miyo, who hung her head and nodded, then walked slowly off the field. Next to the boys, Miyo's mom said something quietly in Japanese. Rocky didn't understand what it was, but he knew she sounded sad.

"What'd he say?" Colt asked as Miyo trudged off the field.

"He says to come back when I learn to catch," Miyo said with a sniff.

"What a jerk," Rocky said angrily.

Miyo's mother put her arm around her daughter's shoulders and gave her a reassuring hug. "Maybe next year, my little butterfly."

"Hey," Rocky said. "I have an idea!" He grabbed his brothers and pulled them off to the side. In a low voice, he said, "What do you say we trade ninja lessons for baseball lessons?"

Tum Tum wrinkled his nose. "You want to take ninja lessons from *a girl?*"

146

"Who cares if she's a girl?" Rocky said. "She's good."

"Well, I don't know," Tum Tum said. He and Rocky turned to Colt to cast the final vote. Colt ran his fingers through his hair.

"Well," he said. "She may be a girl, but she sure beat me."

"Then you'll do it?" Rocky asked eagerly.

"Sure, why not?" Colt said.

Rocky grinned and turned to Miyo. "My brothers and I were wondering if we could make a deal," he said. "You teach us ninja. We teach you baseball."

Miyo's eyes widened, and a smile spread from one corner of her mouth to the other. "That's wonderful!" she cried.

Chapter 11

Meanwhile, high in the black office tower above Tokyo, the door to Koga's private gym opened.

"Unh!"

"Oooof!"

"Ow!"

The three grungers landed in a heap in front of Koga's pool after being thrown into the room by Koga's sumo henchmen.

"You dudes don't have to be so rough!" Glam yelled at them as he got up and dusted himself off.

"Yeah!" shouted Vinnie. "Pick on someone your own size."

"Wrong, dude," Slam said. "They probably can't *find* anyone their own size."

"Shut up," Vinnie snapped.

"No, *you* shut up," Slam replied.

"Silence!" Koga's voice brought the argument to a halt. Glam's uncle got out of the pool and glowered at the grungers, who cowered under his steely glare.

"Where have you been?" Koga demanded.

"Uh, doing your bidding, oh, most respected blood of my blood," Glam answered nervously.

"Then where is the dagger?" Koga asked.

"Uh, we're still working on that, oh, favorite uncle of all my uncles," Glam stammered.

"I am your *only* uncle, fool!" Koga snapped.

"Oh, yeah." Glam grinned sheepishly.

"You haven't brought me the dagger?" Koga asked incredulously.

"Well, not exactly," Glam said, holding up an audiocassette. "But we did bring you this."

As the others watched, Glam stuck the cassette into a tape player and pressed

PLAY. Heavy metal began to boom out of the speakers. The grungers immediately started nodding their heads and swinging their hair.

"All right!" Slam cried. "Rock 'n' roll!"

"Kickin' band, man," Vinnie agreed.

"Smokin'," yelled Glam.

"*Stop!*" Koga shouted over the music. Ishikawa quickly went to the tape player and stopped it.

Koga glared murderously at Glam and his friends. "Why are you wasting my time?"

"Wrong tape," Vinnie said with a shrug as he pulled another cassette out of his pocket. "No big deal."

He put the tape in the tape player, and soon they heard Mori's voice saying, ". . . *take the dagger to Konang for me. And present it to the winner of the competition.*"

"Konang," Koga muttered, rubbing his chin thoughtfully. "So that is his plan. He returns the dagger to the grand master. Perfection. I will be ready for him. Ishikawa, prepare for our journey."

"Hey, what about us, oh, mighty uncle

of Glam?" Vinnie asked. "What about our dough?"

"I asked for the dagger," Koga sneered. "You brought me a tape."

"Well, two tapes, actually," Slam reminded him.

"No payment," Koga said. "You have failed me."

"Hey, we got you a really good lead," Glam said. "That should be worth a couple of bucks."

"You'll get nothing!" Koga shouted. "Ishikawa, take care of them."

Koga stormed out of the gym. The grungers tried to follow, but Ishikawa and the two sumos stepped into their paths. The grungers quickly started to back up.

"Uh, on second thought, we're glad my uncle got the lead," Glam said nervously. "He's right. We don't need to be paid."

Ishikawa and the sumos approached silently.

"In fact, we'll even throw in some more free tapes," Slam added in a quavering voice.

But Koga's henchmen clearly weren't interested.

A moment later the henchmen grabbed them and threw them into the pool.

The boys spent the next two days playing baseball and practicing ninja. Rocky worked hard with Miyo on her catching. Miyo showed Rocky the *kali* exercise called the Art of the Flow, where each partner mirrors the other's movement. She showed Colt how to sharpen his aim with the star-shaped ninja *shirukens*.

Later, Tum Tum taught Miyo more important things about baseball, such as how to spit, tap the dirt out of her cleats with the bat, and blow bubblegum. Miyo took Tum Tum to the sumo school, where he got to dress like a sumo, eat like a sumo, and wear his hair in a sumo bun.

Every morning at precisely seven A.M., Tum Tum's watch beeped, and he and his brothers promptly called home to assure their parents that they were okay.

The night before Grandpa Mori was due to arrive, the boys ate a fish dinner with Miyo and her mom. When they finished, Tum Tum sat back, picking his teeth with a fish bone.

"That was great," he raved. "Hey,

Rocky, tell Miyo's mom how good it was."

Rocky said, *"Subarashi,"* and Miyo's mother nodded graciously.

"Yeah," agreed Tum Tum, *"Super-rushki!"*

Miyo and her mother smiled.

"And that's a real compliment," Colt said, deadpan. "We all know what a picky eater my brother is."

Miyo stood up. "I have a surprise for you." She handed each of the boys a package, which they quickly opened.

"Oh, cool!" Rocky gasped as he and his brothers held up new green, blue, and yellow ninja robes.

"Great, thanks," Colt and Tum Tum chimed in.

"And we have something for you," Rocky said, taking out a box of his own.

"For me?" Miyo's jaw dropped with delight as she opened it and took out a Dragons baseball jersey.

"Oh, thank you!" she squealed.

"Now we'll have something to wear tomorrow when we go back to the *dojo*, and you'll have something to wear for baseball," Rocky said.

Miyo leaned toward Rocky. "Your Japanese is getting better, Rocky," she said. "Maybe you should learn something to say to the grand master tomorrow."

"Yeah," said Tum Tum, "like I strongly suggest you clip your toenails."

Rocky gave Tum Tum a look, but Miyo just giggled.

"I have an idea," she said, standing up and offering Rocky her hand. "Come, I will show you."

Colt winked at Tum Tum as Rocky took Miyo's hand and she led him away from the table. They had both noticed over the past two days that Rocky was starting to get that goofy, mushy look whenever Miyo was around. The same look he got with each girl he fell in love with.

Rocky had been amazed to discover that the walls of Miyo's house were made of nothing more than paper. Miyo led him into her bedroom, although there was no bed, just a *tatami* mat she unrolled each night on the floor. From a shelf filled with books, she took down a Japanese-English text.

"This is the book that helped me learn your language," she said, handing it to him.

Unwilling to put on his glasses in front

of her, Rocky squinted down at the book, unable to read a thing. "Uh, I can't really read Japanese. Maybe you can just teach me a few words."

"But it is half in English," Miyo said, pointing down at the book. "Don't you see?"

"Oh, yeah," Rocky said. "But, uh, could you read it to me? You're better at this than I am."

Miyo smiled and sat down next to Rocky. Their shoulders brushed lightly, and Rocky felt his heart race.

"You go ahead and try," Miyo encouraged him. "Try to sound it out."

Rocky knew he was cornered. He had no choice but to take out his glasses and slip them on. Feeling humiliated and embarrassed, he looked down at the book and started to practice some phrases, saying "hello" and "how are you?" in Japanese.

"Uh, *ohio*," Rocky said. "Is that right?"

Miyo smiled and nodded. "Yes, hello is *ohio*, like the state in your country."

"And, uh, *genki-des-ka?*" Rocky said.

"Very good!" Miyo clapped her hands in delight. "You have just said 'how are you?' in my language."

Rocky smiled, but his mind wasn't on the phrases. He was really wondering how Miyo had reacted to him in glasses.

Finally, curiosity got the better of him, and he glanced in her direction.

Rocky felt his jaw drop, then he grinned. Miyo was also wearing glasses! She must have slipped them on when he wasn't looking! They smiled at each other and moved a little closer. Miyo pointed down at the book and read the next phrase in Japanese. "Happy to meet you."

She moved her face close to his and held his eyes with hers as she softly said, "*Cha-no-yu*."

Rocky felt a stirring inside. He could tell she *really* meant it. He started to take her hand in his, then Colt and Tum Tum suddenly stepped into the room, chanting, "Miyo Shikigawa, Miyo Shikigawa . . ." and leering at them.

"Darn, you guys!" Rocky heaved the book at them.

Miyo just laughed.

The *dojo* was quiet and dark. The only light in the entire building was in the small living quarters of the grand master. He was alone, kneeling before a black lacquer table, preparing for the nightly tea ceremony. Picking up an ornate teapot, he poured the steaming, strong green tea into a small ornate ceramic bowl, then raised it to his lips and sipped.

The grand master took the bowl away from his lips. His forehead wrinkled, then his eyes went wide.

Crash! The bowl fell to the floor as he clutched his throat, and a spasm raced through him. Wracked with sudden pain, and gasping for air, he tried to rise, but only fell over instead and lost consciousness.

From behind a screen, Koga stepped into the room and stood over the inert body of the grand master. He reached down to the floor and lifted up the grand master's blue-and-white mask to his face. The fit was nearly perfect.

Chapter 12

The sun was low and red in the morning sky. The ground was covered with dew. Miyo and the boys walked through the sleeping town and came to the front door of the dojo. Miyo stopped and turned to the boys, who stood by the door holding their ninja bags.

"The grand master says he will start your training today," she said. "Are you nervous?"

Colt shook his head. "We're ready for him. You were a big help."

"And *you* are a big help for my baseball," Miyo said with a smile. She glanced at the great wooden doors of the *dojo* and sighed. "I wish I could go with you."

"Rocky wishes you could go with him, too," Tum Tum said.

Rocky gave his little brother a sharp elbow.

"Ow!" Tum Tum cried.

"Keep it shut," Rocky warned him.

"Well, it's true," Tum Tum complained.

Rocky rolled his eyes and turned back to Miyo.

"Good luck," she said.

"Thanks," said Rocky. There was an awkward moment when neither of them moved. Then Colt whispered something in Rocky's ear.

"Oh, yeah," Rocky said. "Miyo, we want to show you something."

The three brothers put their hands together and invited Miyo to add hers, showing her the "four strands of rope" ritual. Miyo beamed proudly.

"As four strands together we can't be broken," Rocky said. "Don't worry about us. We'll do great. See you later."

"Bye, Miyo." Colt waved.

"Bye, Miyo." Tum Tum also waved, then

added under his breath so she wouldn't hear, "My little chicken pot pie . . ."

"I told you to keep it shut!" Rocky hissed, and took a swing at his little brother. But this time Tum Tum was ready, and ducked.

"Okay, you guys, cut it out," Colt said. "It's time to go in and see the grand master. Get serious."

The boys went in and down the dark hall that led to the main room. Shafts of red sunlight shone through the windows, making them squint. There the grand master met them, wearing his mask and robe. He was accompanied by three ninjas in black uniforms. Each ninja wore a sword. One of them also carried a cellular phone in his belt. The boys bowed.

"So you are the grandsons of Mori Shintaro," the grand master said.

The boys looked up, surprised.

"Hey," said Tum Tum, "how come you didn't speak English to us at the tournament?"

"In front of other people?" the grand master replied sharply. "They would not understand us. It would have been rude.

It is clear that you have much to learn about Japanese customs."

"We are here to learn, sir," Rocky said stiffly.

"Yes," said the grand master. "But first, do you have the dagger your grandfather gave you?"

Again the boys were surprised. "I thought you wanted us to keep it until our grandfather arrived," Colt said.

"I have changed my mind," the grand master informed them. "I want it now."

"Well, okay," Rocky said, nodding at Tum Tum.

Tum Tum opened his bag and began to go through it. At the same time, one of the black ninjas began to draw the curtains over the windows, shutting out the morning sunlight.

Tum Tum thought that was odd, but he continued to rummage through his ninja bag.

"Come on," the grand master said impatiently. "What's taking so long?"

Something wasn't right, and Tum Tum knew it. He glanced down at the bottom of the grand master's robes. *Wait a minute!*

The grand master was wearing shoes with leather tassels. Tum Tum was certain they were too small to contain those big, ugly, callused feet. He took the dagger out and stepped toward the grand master, who extended an eager hand to take it.

"Excuse me," Tum Tum said, holding the dagger just out of his reach. "Weren't you shorter the other day?"

The grand master slouched down, as if trying to make himself shorter.

Suddenly a door swung open on the other side of the room, and Miyo ran in. "Don't give it to him!" she cried. "He's a fake!"

Thinking quickly, Tum Tum reached up with the dagger and cut the strings holding the grand master's mask. The mask fell away, revealing Koga's face.

"After them!" Koga screamed at the black ninjas.

"Scramble!" Tum Tum shouted.

The boys and Miyo ran into the *dojo* gym, where the ninjas practiced skills involving balance and strength. High balance beams spanned the room, as well as climbing ropes and acrobatic rings.

The three black ninjas dashed into the

room and looked around, but the boys and Miyo were nowhere to be found.

"Hee-yaa!" Clinging to climbing ropes, Colt, Rocky, and Miyo swung down from the high balance beams.

Whack! Whack! Whack! They simultaneously kicked the three black ninjas in the head, knocking them backward.

The kids landed on the ground just as the black ninjas jumped to their feet. Two of them pulled out swords. The third yanked out his cellular phone by mistake.

"What are you going to do?" Colt asked as he assumed a fighting position. *"Talk* us to death?"

The black ninja realized his mistake and quickly put back the phone and drew his sword. Miyo, Rocky, and Colt grabbed *bo* sticks from the wall and charged.

Clack! Clank! Bonk! The battle between swords and sturdy *bo* sticks raged. Above them, Tum Tum grabbed a climbing rope and prepared to swing down and join the fight.

Beep . . . beep . . . beep . . . Suddenly his wristwatch began to beep. Oh, no! he thought. It's time to call Mom!

Tum Tum knew he had no choice. If he didn't call her, she'd kill him. But if he tried to call her right now, he was in danger of getting killed anyway. However, faced with the choice of being killed by his mother or a black ninja with a sword, he'd go for the ninja.

There was only one thing to do. Tum Tum grabbed the rope tight and swung down toward the black ninja with the cellular phone tucked in his belt. He grabbed the phone, swung back up onto the high balance beam, and quickly dialed home.

"Oooof!"

"Yeow!"

"Umh!"

The battled raged below. Tum Tum could hardly hear the phone ringing.

"Hey!" he shouted. "You think you guys could hold it down? I'm trying to call my mother."

"Hello?" Jessica answered.

"Oh, hi, Mom," Tum Tum said. "It's me."

"It's about time," his mother said irately. "You're five minutes late."

"Sorry, Mom, I got hung up," Tum Tum said.

Crash! Colt knocked one of the black ninjas through a door.

"What's going on there?" Jessica asked.

"Oh, not much," Tum Tum replied. "You know, we're just in this small town in Japan."

"Are your brothers around?" Jessica asked.

"Oh, yeah, they're around here somewhere," Tum Tum replied.

Rocky and one black ninja were fighting back and forth across the floor below him. The ninja Colt had knocked through the door came charging back out, swinging his sword.

"Let me talk to Colt," Jessica said.

"Uh, okay." Tum Tum put his hand over the cellular phone. "Hey, Colt, Mom wants to talk to you."

In the middle of his battle, Colt looked up. "Well, toss it down," he shouted.

"Comin' down!" Tum Tum tossed the phone to Colt, who caught it with one hand and kept on fighting.

"Hello, Mom?" Colt said. But Jessica had gotten off the phone and their father had gotten on.

"Colt?" Sam said.

"Dad?" Colt gasped.

"Dad?" Rocky looked up nervously.

"Uh-oh," Tum Tum said. "Now we're in trouble."

"Uh, hi, Dad, how was the business trip?" Colt asked as he dodged a slashing sword and delivered a sharp kick to the black ninja's stomach.

"It was fine, thanks." Mr. Douglas sounded mad. "Well, this time you've really done it, haven't you? I thought we'd discussed this. I thought there was going to be no more ninja for a while."

"Oh, uh, we're not doing ninja, Dad," Colt said. "We're just . . . uh, seeing the sights. Meeting people. The regular tourist stuff."

The black ninja attacked again.

Clunk! Colt smacked him on the head with his *bo* stick.

"When you get home we're going to have a long talk about responsibility," Mr. Douglas said sternly. "A *long* talk."

"Uh, fine, Dad," Colt said. "I'll set aside a month."

"Is that sarcasm?" his father asked.

"Uh, no, no, I'm not being sarcastic," Colt said. The black ninja was coming at him again, swinging his sword. Colt realized he'd need two hands to ward off this attack. "Uh, Rocky wants to talk. Bye, Dad."

Colt tossed the phone to Rocky, then spun around and swung his *bo* stick low, knocking the black ninja off his feet.

"Unh! Ahhh!" *Whomp!* The ninja flew up in the air and hit the ground hard.

Meanwhile, in the midst of his own battle, Rocky got on the phone. "Hi, Dad!" He tried to sound cheerful.

"What's all that noise?" Mr. Douglas asked.

"Noise?" Rocky repeated innocently.

"It sounds like fighting," his father said. "You're not in the middle of a fight, are you?"

"Oh, no," Rocky said as he smashed a black ninja in the face with a karate chop. "That's just the TV. We're watching some dumb kung fu movie."

"Eeeeiiii-yaaah!" Miyo let loose one of her screams as she kicked a black ninja in the head.

"What?" his father said. "I can hardly hear you with all that racket. Can't you turn it down?"

"Hey, Tum Tum!" Rocky pretended to shout. "Turn it down! What? The sound's broken?" He got back on the phone. "Sorry, Dad, Tum Tum says the sound is broken."

Rocky's ninja attacked again. The next thing Rocky knew, his *bo* stick was locked against the ninja's sword. Neither of them moved.

"Where's your grandfather?" Mr. Douglas asked.

"Oh, uh, he went fishing with his friends," Rocky said as he strained against the ninja.

"Well, I'd like to speak to him when you call tomorrow," his father said.

"Oh, sure, okay. Could you hold on a second?" Rocky said. The ninja was pressing in on him, and he had bad breath. Rocky had to do something. Suddenly he had an idea and held out the phone. "It's for you."

"Huh?" The black ninja dropped his guard.

Smack! Rocky belted him in the face with the phone.

"Yeiiiii!" The ninja opened his mouth and let out a bloodcurdling cry.

"Gotta go, Dad," Rocky said into the phone. "Bye."

"Mumph!" Rocky shoved the cellular phone into the ninja's mouth.

Briinnng! The cellular phone rang, and the other two black ninjas reached for it. While they were distracted by the phone, Tum Tum snuck up behind them, grabbed the drawstrings of their pants, and pulled.

"Yiiieeee!" The ninjas screamed as their pants fell down around their ankles.

The kids laughed, but only for a second. More black ninjas appeared in the doorway. The kids backed away.

"Uh-oh," Rocky whispered. "They've got friends."

"I know!" Miyo whispered back. "Upstairs!"

The kids turned and raced up the stairs. They reached the top floor, and Miyo pushed open a small, low door.

"Where're you going?" Rocky asked.

"The attic," Miyo said.

"Isn't that kind of a dead end?" Colt asked.

"Trust me," Miyo replied, and ducked inside. The boys glanced at each other.

Thumpa . . . thumpa . . . thumpa . . .
The sound of many footsteps was coming up the stairs behind them.

"I guess we have to trust her," Rocky said, and quickly ducked inside.

The attic ceiling was low, and the boys had to stoop. It was dimly lit and smelled old and musty. No sooner had they gotten inside than two black ninjas climbed in behind them. Bending over severely under the low ceiling, the ninjas crept toward the kids, who backed away.

"I don't like this," Tum Tum whispered nervously.

As the black ninjas came closer, they reached for their swords and tried to pull them out, but the handles banged into the ceiling.

"I just changed my mind," Tum Tum whispered. "Now I like this!"

Rocky and Colt saw their chance. They jumped forward, grabbing the stuck sword handles and swinging on them.

Pow! Pow! They each kicked one ninja hard in the face, then grabbed the swords. As the ninjas fell backward, Rocky and

Colt slashed their initials in the black garments.

"All right!" Tum Tum cheered.

The boys grinned and held up their hands for a high-five with Miyo, but she assumed a karate stance in response.

"No, it's a high-five," Tum Tum tried to explain. "Like this."

"*Ahhhh!*" Miyo stared at him and screamed.

"No, really," Tum Tum said. "It's easy."

"She's screaming at them!" Rocky shouted, pointing past Tum Tum to the doorway.

Tum Tum turned around and saw three more ninjas appear. Miyo jumped in their path and assumed a battle stance.

"*Yi! Yi! Yi!*" Her screams were so shrill that the boys had to cover their ears. The surprised ninjas tumbled backward out of the attic. The three boys stared at her in disbelief.

Miyo looked surprised. "Did I do that?"

"Yeah, but listen," Rocky said. They could hear the sound of more footsteps coming up the stairs.

"This could be a losing proposition," Colt said.

But Miyo shook her head. "Follow me," she whispered.

They followed her to the other end of the attic, where she pulled open a trapdoor.

"This is a secret passageway to outside," she told them.

The boys hurried through it and down a dark winding staircase. Moments later they climbed up a well and into the sunlight. It took a second for their eyes to adjust to the brightness, but when they did, they were in for a surprise.

Koga was standing before them with fifteen henchmen, all aiming guns at Miyo and the boys.

Colt turned to Miyo. "I thought you said it was secret."

"You forget," Koga told Miyo. "I once attended this school."

Rocky could see they were clearly outmanned and outgunned. "What do we do?" he asked the others.

"As I learned here," Koga said, "never enter a battle you can't win."

The man in black signaled his henchmen, who surrounded the kids, took their bags, and led them away.

Chapter 13

They were blindfolded and put in a van and taken someplace. It was impossible to know where, but from the bumpiness of the ride, Rocky suspected it was farther out in the country. There they were taken out of the van and the blindfolds were removed. The air was cool and smelled fresh. The kids looked around and saw that they were surrounded by snowcapped mountains. They were in some kind of camp made up of lots of wooden buildings. Dozens of ninjas were practicing archery or fighting each other with *bo* sticks. The kids were led into a large wooden building. Inside was a gym, where more ninjas were practicing rope climbing and hand-to-hand combat.

"Wow, this is some setup," Colt whispered, obviously impressed.

"Take them downstairs," Koga ordered several guards, including one big guy who had to carry Tum Tum because he wouldn't stop kicking and fighting.

"Let me go!" he yelled. "Let me go, you big ape!"

Downstairs the walls were carved out of rock, and the air was damp and smelled like mildew. The guards led the kids to a cell with iron bars. Inside was a bunkbed, a sink, and a small, barred window. Four large light fixtures hung by chains from the ceiling.

The big guard put Tum Tum down and pulled a plastic bag filled with jelly beans from the boy's pocket.

"Hey!" Tum Tum shouted in dismay as the guard ate a handful and laughed at him. "Did I say ape!" he shouted. "Forget it! It's not fair to the other apes!"

Clang! The guards slammed the cell door shut. Tum Tum slumped onto the bunkbed.

"I think we're in trouble," Rocky said softly as he looked around at the metal bars and stone walls.

"I knew coming to Japan was a bad idea," Tum Tum muttered.

"What?" Colt turned to him, surprised. "You were the one who voted to come here in the first place."

"I just wish I was home," Tum Tum whined. "I want to see Mom and Dad. I want to be in my own house and have a real cheeseburger with real cheese."

"I knew this would get around to food," Colt said with a nod.

Meanwhile, Tum Tum took the crumpled photo of his parents out of his pocket. The boys gazed sadly at it. Suddenly Rocky realized they were feeling sorry for themselves. As if they'd given up.

"Hey," he said, getting up. "What's a ninja?"

"Stop it," Tum Tum said with a sniff. "You're not Grandpa."

But Rocky wouldn't give up. "What is a ninja? A body . . ."

"A spirit," Colt said dispiritedly.

"A mind," said Miyo absently.

Rocky turned to his youngest brother. "Tum Tum?"

"A heart," Tum Tum said with a miserable sigh. He looked so sad that Miyo put her arms around his shoulders and gave him a hug.

Upstairs, Koga pushed through the doors of a small room next to the gym. He was followed by a large sumo in a brown suit. Inside, the three grungers were hanging upside down from the ceiling by their feet.

"Oh, hello, oh, favorite uncle." Glam waved upside down.

"I will give you one last chance," Koga snapped. "I have the dagger and the sword, but they tell me nothing. Only one man knows their secret, and that is Mori Shintaro."

"Who?" Slam asked.

"The old dude," Vinnie whispered.

"Are you capable of kidnapping an old man?" Koga asked. "A hospitalized old man?"

"Uh, if you let us down, oh, fabulous uncle," said Glam, "I have a marvelous idea."

Koga nodded at the sumo, who pulled out a knife and cut the ropes around the grungers' feet.

Thunk! Thunk! Thud! The three grungers fell headfirst to the floor.

Later that day, three new nurses stepped out of the elevator on Grandpa Mori's floor of the hospital. Even in their new white nurses' uniforms and with their hair tucked under cute white nurses' caps, there was something unmistakably ugly and unfeminine about them.

"Wow, dudes, I never realized what freedom of movement a skirt allows," Glam whispered.

"Don't get carried away," Vinnie muttered.

"Whoa, check out the babe!" Slam said as a cute young nurse passed them in the corridor. He started to follow her, but Vinnie grabbed him by the neck.

"You're a nurse, too, dummy," Vinnie reminded him.

"Hey, there he is!" Glam hissed, pointing down the hall. Mori, wearing a hospital gown and wheeling himself in a wheelchair, was coming toward them.

The three grungy nurses quickly stepped behind Mori.

"Uh, sir, would you mind coming with us?" Vinnie asked in a high falsetto as he started to push the wheelchair toward the elevator.

"But I've already had my physical therapy today," Mori protested.

"Uh, this is more in the way of . . ." Vinnie began.

"Discharging you from the hospital," Glam finished the sentence for him as they got into the elevator.

Slam quickly started to fill a syringe from a vial of knockout drops. But as the elevator doors closed, they caught Glam's cap. His silver-white hair spilled out from underneath.

"You!" Mori gasped. He quickly spun the wheelchair around, knocking the grungers off their feet. The elevator doors reopened, and Mori shot out and down the hall.

"Get him!" Glam shouted, and raced after him.

Mori in the wheelchair was no match for the grungers on foot. They raced up behind him and were just about to pounce when an orderly pushed a gurney into the hall.

178

"Ahhhhh!" Slam managed to slide under the gurney, but Glam and Vinnie screamed as they tripped over it and went sliding on their stomach straight into . . . *a huge cart of bedpans!*

Crash! Splash! Clank! The bedpans all tumbled down, dumping their contents all over the two grungers.

Meanwhile, Mori turned a corner and paused to rest. Little did he know that Glam, Slam, and Vinnie had recovered and were sneaking up behind him.

The three grungers charged.

"KEEEEIIII!" Suddenly there was a loud, high-pitched scream and a flash of white as a little old lady in a nurse's uniform jumped out in front of them.

"Nurse Hino!" Mori squeaked.

Whack! Whack! Whack! Nurse Hino delivered three quick punches to the grungers' stomachs, and they went down on their knees.

Nurse Hino stood over them. "You're on the wrong floor, girls. Mine!"

"Ahhhhhhhh!" The grungers jumped up to their feet and went screaming down the hall.

"Whoops!" An orderly was pushing a

rolling bed out of a room and the grungers fell on it and went rolling down the hall . . . straight toward an open window!

"YAAAAAaaaaaaaa!" The bed hit the wall and stopped, but the grungers kept going, right out the window!

Whomp! Whomp! Vinnie and Slam landed side by side on gurneys below.

"Fractured pelvis," Vinnie groaned.

"Hey, good name for a band!" gasped Slam.

CRASH! Glam smashed down onto both of them and the gurneys and grungers collapsed into a heap. A few moments later, Mori wheeled himself out. When he saw the unconscious grungers being wheeled into the emergency room, he smiled.

But not for long . . . Suddenly a thick hand clamped over his mouth as a huge sumo pushed Mori in his wheelchair toward a black van. Ishikawa held open the door, and the sumo lifted the wheelchair with Mori in it and put them inside. Ishikawa slammed the door shut and quickly drove off.

Later the van rolled into Koga's mountain compound. Mori was taken out of the van and pushed into a dark office. Ishikawa stood nearby with a gun to make sure the old man didn't try to escape.

Mori had never seen a place so opulently decorated with gold statues and ivory elephant tusks. Whoever owned this place was not only very rich, but wanted everyone to know it.

"Why have you brought me here?" he demanded, but Ishikawa remained silent.

Then a door opened, and a man in black stepped into the room. "Go, Ishikawa," he said. "I will continue."

Mori stared at the man. They were about the same age, but he did not recognize him. "Who are you?" he asked.

"Just a boy," Koga replied with a sinister smile.

"What?" Mori was puzzled.

Koga came closer and took out the dagger. He stroked Mori's cheek with its point. "A boy you once knew in Konang."

Mori looked more closely. Now he could see the scar on the man's cheek.

"Koga?" he gasped.

"Yes."

"So this is what has become of you," Mori

said, looking around the office again. "I remember well your greed."

"I think you remember more," Koga said. "I have the sword and your dagger. But the cave of gold, Mori. Where is it?"

"The cave?" Mori shook his head. "That was just a story. A story to entertain little boys."

Koga squinted and pressed the point of the dagger against Mori's cheek. "Entertain this little boy. Or would you like a souvenir on your face like the one you gave me?"

Mori said nothing.

Koga pointed to the scar on his face. "The day I received this, I pledged to own that treasure, and now I will have it."

"The little boy I knew had some decency in him," Mori said. "But now you have wealth beyond a lifetime of spending. Why do you want more?"

"Maybe I'm just fulfilling a little boy's dream," Koga replied with a leer.

"I'm sorry, Koga." Mori shook his head. "I can't help you. I remember nothing about the cave."

"Then I will help you remember," Koga snarled.

Mori braced himself, expecting some

kind of terrible blow, but instead Koga grabbed him by the shoulder, pulled him up out of the wheelchair, and out of the room.

A few moments later, the kids heard a door slam and were stunned to see Mori stumbling toward their cell with Koga and some sumos following behind.

"Grandpa!" they cried, jumping up.

"Boys!" Mori was surprised and disappointed to find them in the cell. "Are you all right?"

"We're okay," Rocky said.

"What about you?" Colt asked. "They're not hurting you, are they?"

"Get us out, Grandpa!" Tum Tum cried, grabbing the bars. "Please!"

"I'll do my best," Grandpa Mori assured them. "Who's that with you?"

"Rocky's girlfriend," Tum Tum said.

"She is not!" Rocky snapped, but then Miyo gave him a disappointed look and he changed his tune. "Well, er, I mean . . ."

"Don't worry," Grandpa Mori said. "I will get you out. Remember, four strands of rope."

The three boys pressed their hands together. Miyo added hers as the fourth strand.

Clang! Suddenly Mori was smashed facefirst into the bars as Koga struck him from behind.

"The cave!" the man in black shouted. "Where is the cave?"

Mori shook his head, and Koga pressed his lips close to the old man's ear.

"Do you wish to watch your grandchildren die?" he whispered.

Mori thought fast. "According to the legend," he said, "the cave is beneath Castle Hikone. The sword and the dagger are the keys. Now let my grandchildren go."

Koga pulled Mori away from the cell. "You'll go to Castle Hikone first," he snarled, pushing the old man ahead of him down the hall.

"Grandpa!" the kids yelled behind him.

As Koga left, he stopped beside one of his sumo henchmen and whispered, "Tell the guards to eliminate the kids after I've reached the treasure."

The sumo nodded and looked back at the kids with an evil grin.

Chapter 14

The kids sat in the cell, wondering what would happen next. Tum Tum watched the guard who was seated in a chair in the hall, reading a Japanese comic book and munching on his jelly beans. Colt studied the stone walls. Rocky looked up at the small barred window.

"A ninja must be able to use everything around him to his advantage," Colt said.

"But there's nothing here we can use," Tum Tum complained.

Colt reached into his pocket and took out a small silver ball. "I still have a *pachinko* ball."

"Whooppee!" Tum Tum said sourly. "I don't even have my jelly beans anymore. Forget it. There's no way to escape."

Rocky stared up at the four light fixtures hanging by chains. Maybe there was a way . . .

"Hey," he whispered. "Maybe we don't have to escape. Maybe we just have to make it *look* like we did."

"How?" Tum Tum asked.

Rocky winked and moved close to the bars. "Get the sheets off the bed and tie them together," he said loudly. "We'll make a rope."

"But that won't work," Tum Tum said, pointing up at the window. "We'll never get through that window. The bars are too close together.

Rocky glared at his youngest brother and then whispered, *"Just play along."*

"I get it," Miyo said. Then more loudly she added, "Okay, tie one end to the bed."

Rocky managed to remove a small piece of pipe from under the sink. "Careful, everyone," he said loudly as he reached up to the window. "Stand back."

Crash! He broke the window with the pipe.

"Let's get the sheet out the window," Miyo said.

With one end of the sheet tied to the bed, the kids began to feed the other end through the narrow bars and out the window. Out of the corner of his eyes, Rocky saw the guard get up and check on what they were doing. But when he saw how narrow the spaces between the window bars were, he just shook his head and laughed. Then he sat down again and started to read the comic book.

"Okay, Colt," Rocky said loudly. "You first. Be careful . . . You next, Tum Tum. Hurry up . . ."

"I'm hurrying," Tum Tum said.

Rocky watched the guard shake his head and smile again as he continued to read the comic.

Finally Rocky said, "Okay, I'll go last. See you down below."

The cell became silent. The guard looked up. It was empty! The guard jumped up and looked through the bars. The kids were gone! The sheet rope was hanging out the window. How in the world? He quickly took out his key, unlocked the cell door, and stepped inside.

"Hi-yaa!" Rocky shouted.

The startled guard looked up just in time to see Rocky's feet plummeting down toward him.

Whomp! Rocky kicked the guard, knocking him out cold. The guard slumped unconscious to the floor, and the kids climbed down from the light fixtures, where they'd been hanging. Rocky and the others headed out through the open cell door. Tum Tum reached into the guard's pocket and removed his bag of jelly beans.

"Don't you just hate us?" he asked with a smile.

"Come on, Tum Tum," Colt said. "We gotta find Grandpa."

Suddenly they heard footsteps. Two of Koga's henchmen were coming down the stairs. At just the right moment, Tum Tum rolled a handful of jelly beans under their feet.

"Yiii!" The bad guys slipped and fell.

But instead of running, Tum Tum bent down to pick up his jelly beans.

"What are you doing?" Rocky gasped.

"Well, you don't expect me to leave them, do you?" Tum Tum asked.

By now the bad guys had gotten back on their feet.

Thunk! Thunk! Rocky and Colt kicked them away while Miyo grabbed Tum Tum and led him down the hall. They ran upstairs and encountered two more henchmen. Rocky and Miyo grabbed fire extinguishers from the wall and sprayed both men in the face. Then knocked them out with kicks. They hurried down the hall and came to an office.

"This must be Koga's office," Rocky said.

Colt pushed open the door, ready to fight. But the room was empty. "They're not here."

"They are going to the castle already," Miyo said.

"Look, our bags!" Rocky shouted, pointing at their ninja bags piled up in a corner. The boys grabbed them.

"We have to get to the castle!" Colt shouted.

"I know how to go!" said Miyo, leading them out of the room.

On the way out of the room, Tum Tum

spotted a bowl of fruit and stopped to dump it into his bag.

"Tum Tum!" Colt shouted impatiently. "You pig!"

"But it's health food!" Tum Tum protested, and followed the others out of the room.

They ran outside, but a group of ninjas practicing hand-to-hand combat spotted them.

"Quick!" Rocky shouted, grabbing an archery bow and tossing several to the others.

"But the arrows are locked up!" Miyo cried as she tried to open a wooden box.

"Use these!" Tum Tum yelled, tossing fruit out of his bag to the others. The kids quickly fired the fruit at the approaching ninjas, pelting them with apples, bananas, oranges, and pineapples.

Now more ninjas arrived.

"I'm running out of fruit!" Tum Tum shouted.

"Back inside!" Rocky yelled, waving the kids back into the dojo.

The kids ran into the gym and started to fill their bags with *nunchakus, shirukens,* and other weapons. Suddenly ninjas began to pour in through several doors.

"The roof!" Miyo shouted, guiding the boys through a doorway that led to the stairs.

Thump! Thump! Thump! A huge sumo was clomping down the stairs toward them. Meanwhile, a crowd of ninjas was climbing up from behind. The kids were trapped!

"Got any ideas?" Colt asked.

Rocky and Miyo shook their heads.

"Come on, you guys, use your imaginations," Tum Tum quipped. He quickly ran through the sumo's legs. The sumo bent over and looked through his legs. Tum Tum now stood behind him. It was just too tempting. He took aim and *whop!* kicked him with both feet.

The sumo started to lose his footing. Colt and Rocky quickly grabbed him by the arms and pulled.

Ka-boom! The sumo went flying down the stairs and crashed into the crowd of ninjas coming up, flattening every one of them.

"All right!" The kids gave each other high-fives and continued up to the roof.

"Look out!" Tum Tum cried.

Rumbling toward them were two more huge sumos.

"Light up their eyes!" Rocky shouted.

The boys immediately attacked the sumos, using the moves they'd practiced on the dummy back at Grandpa Mori's cabin.

Thud! Colt and Miyo knocked one down easily.

Whap! Whap! Whap! Tum Tum hit the second sumo three times, but the big man kept coming.

"Remember what Grandpa said," Rocky yelled. "You get something easier when you don't want it."

"I don't want to hit him," Tum Tum told himself. "I don't want to hit him."

Crunch! Tum Tum hit the sumo with all his might. The sumo staggered backward, and Tum Tum jumped on his shoulders and locked his legs around the man's huge neck.

"*YAAA . . . mphmmm!*" The sumo opened his mouth to yell, but Tum Tum quickly pulled an apple out of his bag and stuffed it into the man's mouth.

Thud! The sumo fell backward partway off the roof. He was out cold. From his waist onward he was sticking out into the air! Tum Tum found himself hanging upside down in the air with his legs still wrapped around the huge man's neck. He knew if he let go, he'd fall four stories straight down.

"Help! Help!" he shouted.

"Form a chain!" Rocky yelled. Colt stayed on the roof and held Miyo's ankles. Miyo held Rocky's ankles as he crawled over the unconscious sumo toward his little brother. Finally he grabbed Tum Tum's ankles.

"Let go, Tum Tum!" he shouted.

"Are you crazy?" Tum Tum shouted back.

"I said let go!" Rocky yelled again.

"Nooooo!"

"Let! GO!" Rocky shouted with all his might.

Tum Tum let go, and Rocky swung him up onto the roof. Then Colt and Miyo pulled Rocky back to safety. The kids barely had time to catch their breaths before they heard footsteps charging up the stairs to the roof. Miyo ran to the roof door and slammed it shut, swinging a thick piece of wood over the latches to stop anyone from breaking through.

"Now what?" Colt asked.

Rocky ran over to the edge of the roof and looked down. "Too high to jump," he said.

"I could have told you that," Tum Tum said.

Meanwhile, Miyo was pointing to something in the distance.

"There," she yelled. "That is Castle Hikone."

"Great," Colt said. "We're here and Grandpa Mori's over there."

"We have to get there," Rocky said.

"Yeah, right," snapped Tum Tum. "We can't even get off this roof. How're we gonna get all the way over there?"

"I guess we fly," Miyo said with a smile.

"Huh?" Colt and Tum Tum looked at her as if she were crazy, but Miyo pointed at another part of the roof where two hang gliders lay.

"All right!" Rocky let out a cheer and led them toward the gliders.

"I'll strap you in," Miyo told Colt and Tum Tum as they lifted the first glider up.

"We're really gonna fly?" Tum Tum gulped nervously.

"Glide," Colt corrected him. "We're gonna glide."

"Yeah, but I mean, how?" Tum Tum asked. "We can't just stand on the edge of the roof and jump."

"You have to take a running start," Rocky said as he and Miyo strapped themselves into the other glider. "That'll give you enough momentum to catch an updraft."

"Listen to Mr. Hang-Gliding Expert," Tum Tum groaned, rolling his eyes. "When did you get so smart?"

"I read about it in a magazine," Rocky explained.

"Oh, great," Tum Tum groaned. "Now I feel *really* confident."

Boom! Boom! Creak! Across the roof came the sound of banging and wood splintering.

"They're starting to break down the door!" Colt yelled.

"Time to go!" Rocky yelled.

Colt started to run, but Tum Tum dragged his feet.

"What are you doing?" Colt gasped.

"Listen," Tum Tum said. "I really don't think I can do this."

"Oh, grow up!" Colt snapped.

"This has nothing to do with growing up," Tum Tum told him. "I just don't think I can do it."

Crash! Behind them the roof door gave way, and a crowd of ninjas and sumos charged through.

"Time to go!" Rocky shouted. The two hang-gliding teams started to run.

"Faster!" Colt yelled.

"I can't look!" Tum Tum cried as they approached the edge of the roof.

"Jump!" Miyo shouted.

Colt launched himself and his little brother into the air.

"*Ahhhhhhh!*" Tum Tum screamed as his feet left the roof and the hang glider took flight.

The setting sun was turning red in the evening sky. Miyo and Rocky glided together over the Japanese countryside in the peaceful, warm air. Castle Hikone loomed ahead, but it would be a little while until they reached it. In the meantime, Rocky appreciated this restful moment with Miyo. Their shoulders rubbed together as they flew. Rocky smiled at Miyo, and she smiled back.

"This is nice," Rocky said.

"Yes," Miyo agreed.

"Maybe someday we'll get to do it again," Rocky said.

"That would be nice," said Miyo.

"But next time we'll leave those guys at home," Rocky said, gesturing over his shoulder at his brothers.

"Okay." Miyo nodded.

"That way it'll be a little quieter," Rocky said.

"*Ahhhhhhhhhhhh!*" Tum Tum's scream continued to pierce the calm of the evening.

"Are you gonna scream all the way to Castle Hikone?" Colt asked.

"*Yeeeeessssssss!*" Tum Tum screamed.

"It's really hurting my ears," Colt complained.

"*Soooorrrrrrryyyyy!*"

"Can't you at least try to stop?"

"Nooooooooooo!"

"I really don't see what the big deal is," Colt said. "It's just like a roller coaster."

"I hate roller coasterssssssss!" Tum Tum screamed.

Chapter 15

It was night by the time Koga and his men reached Castle Hikone. The dark castle loomed ominously in the dull moonlight. Koga got out of his limousine and yanked Mori out. Ishikawa and half a dozen henchmen followed from their black van.

Moonlight glistened on the still water in the moat that surrounded the castle. Koga pointed to two of his men.

"You two," he shouted. "Stand guard."

Then he turned to Mori and said, "We have the sword and the dagger, the keys to the treasure. Now where is the door?"

Mori pressed his lips together in silence.

Koga stepped closer, brandishing the ancient samurai sword.

"I will kill you as quick as you can breathe," he threatened. "And then I will kill your grandchildren."

Mori took a deep, reluctant breath. "The legend spoke of an entranceway near the moat."

Koga stared at the still, black water. On the near side of the moat stood an old well. It seemed like an odd place for a well. Then Koga had an idea.

"There!" he yelled, pointing at the well. "Try there."

Koga's men hurried to the well and looked down it. One of the men waved.

"*Hai!*" he called back to Koga in Japanese. "There's a ladder."

Koga turned to Mori and smiled wickedly. "Do I remember you saying it was just a legend? Something to amuse little boys?"

Mori shrugged.

"Come on, Mori," Koga sneered, grabbing him by the shoulder. "Let's go see where this little boy's story leads."

Together with Ishikawa and four henchmen, Koga led Mori into the well and down the ladder. Ishikawa carried a flashlight and led the way.

Behind them, the two men Koga had left as guards stood fifty yards apart in the dark. Neither noticed as Rocky and Miyo landed softly in the grass behind them.

Meanwhile, Colt and Tum Tum were coming in for a more difficult landing.

"Look out!" Tum Tum whispered hoarsely. *"You're heading for that tree!"*

"Lean!" Colt whispered back.

"I can't," Tum Tum hissed. *"I'll fall off!"*

"You can't fall off, dummy. You're strapped in!"

But it was too late.

Crackle . . . snap! They crashed into the tree.

On the ground, one of Koga's guards heard the rustling of branches and went to investigate. As the guard approached the tree, Colt grabbed Tum Tum by the ankles and swung him down. The guard looked up . . .

Clunk! Tum Tum bashed him in the face with a quick punch, and the guard went down.

"Can we go down now?" Tum Tum asked in a low voice.

"Yes," his brother replied.

Tum Tum quickly scampered down the tree, then kneeled on the ground and pressed his face into the grass.

"What are you doing?" Colt asked.

"Kissing the ground," Tum Tum replied.

A few moments later, the second guard rejoined the first. It appeared that he'd grown slightly taller, although in the dark it was hard to really tell.

The first guard took out a cigarette. In Japanese he asked, "Do you have a light?"

"Ninjas don't smoke, doofus," Tum Tum answered. Inside the second guard's uniform he was sitting on Colt's shoulders. Now his leg shot out of the guard's jacket as he caught the first guard squarely in the stomach.

"*Oooooooiiieeee!*" The guard's eyeballs bulged out and his jaw dropped. His knees buckled and he staggered backward.

Pow! Colt gave him a shot to the chest.

Splash! The guard fell backward into the moat.

"*Whoa!*" Colt's kick threw them off balance and he and Tum Tum tumbled to the ground.

"You guys okay?" Rocky asked as he and Miyo ran out of the shadows.

"Yeah," Colt said. He and Tum Tum pulled off the second guard's clothes. "But we could have used some help."

"Yeah," Tum Tum leered. "Where *were* you two?"

Miyo glanced at Rocky and bit her lip. Rocky blushed. Good thing it was dark and his brothers couldn't tell.

The well led to a tunnel under the moat. As they walked, Ishikawa flashed the light on the walls, illuminating ancient Japanese paintings of samurai warriors and beautiful maidens.

But soon the passageway came to an end, and the small search party found themselves facing a wall of solid rock. They watched as Ishikawa traced the corners with the flashlight, looking for a way to proceed.

"You see?" Mori said. "It goes nowhere. Just to a wall."

Thump! Koga slammed his fist against the cold gray rock. "No! I will find it!"

"There is nothing to find," Mori said.

"Shut up!" Koga snapped. He was staring at something on the wall. It appeared to be part of another old painting. The man in black reached up and brushed away the dust, revealing more of the painting. Now he could see it clearly. It was a painting of two warriors in battle. One held a sword, the other a dagger. Koga smiled. The sword and dagger were identical to the ones he carried.

He leaned closer and suddenly saw a slot in the stone wall beside the painting of the sword. The slot was filled with centuries of dust and grime. Koga carefully brushed it away with his finger.

"And now for the dagger," he said softly. Within the drawing of the dagger, he found another slot and cleared that one, too.

"So . . ." Koga smiled to himself. "This *is* the gate to my cave of gold."

Koga took out the sword and slid it into the first slot. Then he took out the dagger and slid it into the second slot.

Creak! came the sound of ancient gears turning. The solid stone wall in front of them shook, and a fine mist of dust fell away. The wall began to move slowly until a narrow opening was visible.

Koga grabbed the flashlight away from Ishikawa and eagerly shined it inside, revealing a stone passageway.

"Just a story to entertain little boys," he muttered with a smile and turned to Mori. "What do you think now?"

"I think it has not been disturbed for a long time," Mori said. "Perhaps that is the way it was meant to be."

Koga frowned. "Who cares what you think?" he snapped, pointing into the dark passage. "Inside!"

The stone passageway was narrow and low. Koga and the others had to duck as they walked through it. The air felt cold and strangely still, as if it was unwilling to be disturbed after so many centuries. Mori felt a chill and knew it wasn't just the cool temperature. There were spirits here who resented this intrusion.

The passageway led to an ancient underground room with walls and a ceiling of stone. In the center of the room was a long wooden table. As Koga swept the flashlight beam over it, Mori gasped. Seated all around the table were skeletons! Their heads and arms were lying over ancient settings of wooden plates and cups, as if they'd died in the midst of a feast.

It would be wise to leave this place as quickly as possible, Mori told himself, but it was not possible, given the circumstances. He glanced around the rest of the room. At one end a huge hanging panel on rope pulleys hid the wall behind it from view. At the other end stood a decrepit crumbling old shrine with a religious statue of an ancient god.

Koga surveyed the scene with grim determination. Four ancient torches hung at angles from the walls.

"Light the torches," he ordered one of his men, who quickly went around the room with a lighter. Flames burst from the torches, filling the room with eerie, flickering light that made the shadows of the skeletons dance against the walls.

If Koga was unnerved by the sight before him, he didn't show it. But Mori couldn't resist pointing out that this could not have been what the man in black expected.

"Here are your treasures, Koga," he said. "Look! An ancient crumbling shrine. Nothing but skulls and bones."

"Liar!" Koga shouted, spinning around and slapping Mori in the face. "The cave is in here! I can feel it!"

Koga whipped the flashlight around the room, searching for something that would lead to the cave. "There!" he shouted, pointing to a corner of the room. "Those stairs!"

He quickly led his men to a stone stairway in the corner of the room.

"It goes down," Ishikawa said, staring into the dark depths below.

"Wait here, Ishikawa," Koga ordered, and led Mori and the remaining four henchmen down the dark stairs.

Meanwhile the kids had climbed down the well ladder and entered the underground passageway. Colt led the way with a small penlight he'd taken from his pocket.

"Uh, I don't like the looks of this place," Tum Tum said, glancing nervously at the ancient painted figures on the wall.

"All I know is that Koga creep must've taken Grandpa down here," Colt said.

"Well, maybe we ought to go back out and wait for them outside," Tum Tum suggested hopefully.

"I'm not so sure Grandpa would come back out," Rocky said. "Koga needs him to find the treasure. Once he finds it, he's not gonna need Grandpa anymore."

"But he wouldn't just leave Grandpa down here," Tum Tum said.

The others turned and glared at him.

"Uh, on second thought, he probably would," Tum Tum admitted.

"Hey, look!" Colt gasped. He stood down at the end of the passageway, shining his penlight against the wall.

"The sword and the dagger!" Rocky gasped.

"Why are they stuck in the wall?" Miyo asked.

"Remember Koga said something about them being the keys to finding the treasure?" Rocky asked. "I guess he really meant it."

"What do you think is down there?" Colt asked, pointing his penlight into the secret passage behind the stone wall.

"I don't know, but I guess we're gonna find out," Rocky said, reaching for the handle of the sword.

"Maybe you should leave them there," Colt said.

"No, we may need them," Rocky replied, pulling the sword out of the stone. Tum Tum pulled out the dagger. He opened a secret Velcro compartment on the bottom of his ninja bag and slid the dagger inside.

"Uh, you first," Colt said to Rocky, handing the penlight to him.

"Okay, guys, here goes." Rocky took a deep breath to steady his nerves and stepped into the secret passageway behind the stone wall.

Creak! Thump! No sooner had they all gone through the opening than the stone wall closed behind them.

"Oh, great," Colt pressed against it and groaned. "It's sealed shut!"

"Nice going, spaz," Miyo said.

"Why do I have the feeling that's the kind of door that only locks from the outside?" Tum Tum asked with a moan.

"Come on," Rocky said, heading down the passageway. "We'll worry about it later."

"Only an optimist would say that," Tum Tum said with a sigh.

The kids went down the passageway and entered the ancient dining room, lit by the flickering torches.

"Whoa!" Tum Tum's eyes went wide when he saw the skeletons. "Remind me not to eat here anytime soon."

"What is this place?" Rocky asked.

"It's creepy, that's what it is," Tum Tum said.

"Man, these guys must've eaten something that really disagreed with them," Colt said, staring at the skeletons.

"Is some kind of ancient shrine, I think," Miyo said.

"Either that or it's part of a fast-food chain that really bombed," said Tum Tum.

"Hey, look!" Colt pointed at the staircase in the corner. "There must be another level."

"All these levels," Tum Tum groaned. "I'm starting to feel like a Mario Brother."

"You're starting to *look* like one, too," Colt added, patting his little brother's stomach.

"Well, something tells me they went

thataway," Rocky said, pointing at the stairs. "So I guess we'll go, too."

The kids hurried toward the stairs. Suddenly Ishikawa stepped out before them.

"*Ahhhhhhh!*" the kids screamed and jumped back.

Ishikawa smiled menacingly and took his time removing his jacket for battle.

Rocky hurled the samurai sword at him, but with a flick of his wrist, Ishikawa caught the sword by the blade and started to advance toward them.

The kids backed away. Rocky stumbled backward into one of the skeletons, which instantly fell apart with a loud clatter. Suddenly Rocky had an idea. He picked up the skull and threw it at the man in the white suit.

Clang! Using the samurai sword as a bat, Ishikawa knocked the skull away.

Clang! Clang! He knocked away skulls thrown by Tum Tum and Miyo, too.

Miyo leaped up and made a great one-handed catch.

"Nice catch, Miyo!" Rocky shouted as she held the skull up proudly.

"*Look out, Rocky!*" Colt shouted.

Rocky turned just in time to see Ishikawa hurl the sword back at him. He instantly did a ninja backflip.

Sproing! the sword lodged itself in the ancient wooden banquet table, giving Rocky an idea.

"Colt! Tum Tum!" He waved them over to the table. Together they started to lift it.

Meanwhile, Miyo ran up to Ishikawa and assumed an attack position, giving her trademark scream: *"Iiiieee-yah!"*

Ishikawa instantly assumed a fighting stance and unleashed an even mightier scream: *"IIIIIEEEEE-YAHHOY!"*

"Uh-oh . . ." Miyo was momentarily startled, but quickly followed with a barrage of kicks and punches.

Ishikawa only laughed as he fended them off.

"Miyo, look out!" Rocky shouted as he and his brothers rushed at the man in white, using the table as a battering ram. Miyo tumbled out of the way and the boys charged.

Crash! Ishikawa met the table with an incredible head butt. The old table splintered into a hundred pieces, leaving each of the boys with some planks of wood in their hands.

"Guess you could say he really used his head," Tum Tum observed.

"I guess we'll use what we've got," Rocky said, holding up the plank of wood in his hand.

"*Hiii-yah!*" The kids all attacked at once. Ishikawa quickly disposed of Tum Tum with a swift kick, then grabbed the other kids and threw them against the wall. As Rocky hit the wall, a door near him opened. He looked inside and got an idea.

"Huddle!" he yelled.

The kids gathered around him and he quickly explained his plan. A moment later, Rocky, Tum Tum, and Colt slid inside the door and closed it.

Miyo stepped in front of the door and started to taunt Ishikawa.

"You're a stupid hippo!" she said in Japanese. "A stupid clown! And your mother's belly button sticks out!"

Ishikawa's eyes narrowed, and he clenched and unclenched his fists.

"If you have a mother," Miyo taunted.

"Maybe you were just hatched from an egg."

Ishikawa's eyes widened, and his face darkened.

"YYIIIEEEE-HOYYYYY!" He charged Miyo like a raging bull.

At the last second, Miyo stepped out of the way and opened the door.

CRUNCH! Ishikawa crashed into a solid stone wall inside the door. Tum Tum quickly crawled out from beneath his legs. Rocky and Colt slid out from small spaces on either side.

Bang! Miyo quickly slammed the door, leaving Koga's henchman inside.

"Guess it's time to see what's down there," Rocky said, heading for the next stairs.

"You *sure* you want to go down there?" Tum Tum asked.

Rocky stopped at the entrance to the stairs and looked down. Suddenly he saw something.

"On second thought," he said, quickly backing away. "Maybe it's not such a good idea."

"You changed your mind?" Tum Tum asked, amazed.

"I didn't change my mind," Rocky replied. *"They* did!"

Just at that moment, Koga's four henchmen raced up the stairs, brandishing their swords.

The kids backed away, pulling razor-sharp *shirukens* from their bags.

Zip! Zip! Whizzzz! The *shirukens* shot through the air, but the henchmen ducked and returned fire with *shirukens* of their own. The kids ducked behind the ancient shrine. Lying behind it was an old ladder made of thin logs tied with rope to two long poles. Rocky looked up at the walls and noticed a thin ledge high on the wall and circling the room.

"Come on!" he shouted to the others.

He and Colt pushed the ladder against the wall. The kids started to climb up, with Rocky going last. As he passed the eighth rung, he kicked it.

Crack! The rung cracked, but didn't break. Rocky followed the others up on the ledge.

Koga's henchmen raced after them. The first one went up the ladder, followed by the others, but as he grabbed the eighth rung, it snapped.

Crack! Crack! Crack! Crack! The top henchman slid back down the ladder, breaking all the rungs beneath him and crashing into the others.

"Next time try the elevator!" Rocky shouted from the ledge above.

"Rocky!" Miyo suddenly screamed.

Rocky turned and saw that the stone ledge under Miyo's feet had started to crumble. He grabbed her arm and pulled her back a split second before she would have fallen.

"Guess we can't go any farther *that* way," Tum Tum said.

Meanwhile, Koga's henchmen were climbing up on each other's shoulders to reach the ninth rung of the ladder. The top one grabbed it and began to climb up toward the ledge. Rocky quickly slipped off one of his shoes and held it over the top of the ladder.

As the climber reached the top, he saw Rocky's shoe above him and grabbed it. But instead of getting a foot and leg, he got an empty shoe.

"Shoe department, lower level!" Rocky yelled.

"*Ahhhhh!*" the top climber fell backward and crashed once again into his partners.

Above them on the ledge, the kids smiled, but not for long. Koga's henchmen quickly regrouped and formed a human ladder, crawling up one another until the top one reached the ledge to Rocky's right. Rocky looked to his left, but that was the spot where the ledge had crumbled under Miyo.

The henchman stood up on the ledge, pulled out his sword, and started to approach.

"Uh-oh," Tum Tum whimpered. "We're stuck!"

The kids were trapped on the ledge, and Koga's henchmen were coming closer. Colt was closest to the henchmen. The lead man drew his sword and swung. Colt backed up.

Clank! The sword struck the wall.

"Colt!" Rocky cried, "if you back up anymore, you'll push us off the ledge."

"What do you expect me to do?" Colt shouted back as the lead henchman came closer.

"I don't know," Rocky yelled. "Think of something."

The henchman came closer, pulling his sword back to strike. Colt knew he had a choice: He could back up and force the others off the ledge, or he could just stand there and get skewered by the sword.

Or . . . He had an idea and quickly stamped his foot down on the ledge.

Crunk! The ledge started to give.

Colt kicked it again and again.

CRUNK! The ledge fell away. The lead henchman started to back away.

"Oooof!" He backed into the others.

"Ahhhhhh!" They all tumbled to the floor.

Colt turned to the others and smiled. "How's that for ninja-nuity?"

"Pretty good," Tum Tum said.

"Except . . ." Rocky pointed at the ledge beneath them. Now it, too, was starting to crumble.

"Ahhhhhh!" Expecting to fall any second, they all screamed. But instead of falling down, they fell *back* as the wall behind them suddenly folded away like a revolving door.

A split second later, the kids disappeared.

Chapter 16

Koga and Mori were now alone. They'd come to a cold stone cavern. Koga bent down and picked up something from the floor: another torch! Mori was tired of this game. He didn't like treading in these dark, sacred places. One way or another, he wanted to get out.

"You're chasing fairy tales!" he told Koga. "And I'm not going to be buried here for your greed."

Koga was busy trying to light the torch. Mori sensed that Koga would not expect him to charge, so that's what he did. Just at that second, Koga got the torch lit. He swung the flaming stick at Mori.

Suddenly both men stopped. The walls of the cave were illuminated by the torch, and Mori and Koga looked around in wonder as the torch's light was reflected back at them by the cave's walls. *Walls of solid gold!* With intricate patterns carved into them. A carving of a huge dragon encircled the entire room, and at its feet ninja warriors battled. Mori couldn't believe his eyes. He had never seen anything so fabulous and beautiful.

"Ha!" Koga laughed triumphantly. "Here is your fairy tale, Mori Shintaro!"

"The legend was true!" Mori gasped in amazement.

Across the room, Koga pulled a gun out of his jacket. "Your job is complete, old friend. Say your prayers before you join the dead."

Mori knew he had only one chance: He fell to his knees before Koga and clasped his hands. "I beg you, Koga."

Koga stepped closer and smirked. "Can I believe my eyes? Is this the great warrior Mori Shintaro begging for his life?" Koga aimed the gun at him. "Good-bye, Mori."

Swipe! Mori reached out, grabbed Koga's leg and flipped him backward. The gun clattered to the ground.

Whack! As Koga scrambled to his feet, Mori delivered a sharp kick. Koga tumbled backward.

"I beat you once, Koga," Mori said, assuming a ninja stance and preparing for the fight of his life.

"That was a long time ago, Grandpa!" Koga grinned menacingly and faced him.

The kids were sliding down a smooth stone chute in the dark. They grabbed desperately at the walls, trying to latch onto something to halt their downward progress.

"Where's this going?" Colt yelled.

"How would we know?" Rocky yelled back.

"I *still* hate roller coasters!" Tum Tum yelled.

In the golden chamber, the two old men were locked in a fierce battle for control of the gun. They rolled across the floor for it. Koga managed to pick it up, but Mori grabbed his hand to stop him from aiming it.

"Still greedy, Koga!" Mori gasped as they fought. "For gold or glory at school — it was always your weakness! I will win, Koga, because you are controlled by your greed."

"Talk as much as you like," Koga hissed as he slowly forced the barrel of the gun toward Mori. "Talk now and then forever hold your peace."

Koga had the position of greater leverage. Another few seconds and he would be able to pull the trigger.

"*Ahhhhhh!*" A gold panel in the wall behind them suddenly opened and the kids fell through it, smashing into Mori and Koga, and knocking the gun from Koga's hand.

BANG! There was a bright flash and a loud explosion. The gun accidentally fired as Koga lost his grip on it.

Ruummmmmbbbbbllllleeee . . .

Suddenly the room began to shake, and dust and small bits of dirt began to fall.

"Look!" Colt pointed up at the ceiling. "The ceiling's starting to cave in!"

"Let's go!" Mori shouted.

"You mean, scramble!" yelled Tum Tum. Everyone jumped to their feet at the same time.

The kids and Mori began to run toward the stairs, but Koga stayed behind, as if he couldn't bring himself to part with the gold.

"It's not worth it, Koga!" Mori shouted at him.

Still, Koga hesitated.

"If you were a real ninja you wouldn't care about the gold," Rocky yelled back at him.

Koga seemed to waver. He gave Mori a grim look. "You have taught your grandsons well, Mori. They are very honorable."

"You were once honorable, too," Mori said solemnly. "Fifty years ago I accidentally scarred your face. But it is what happened to your soul that I truly regret."

For a second, Koga touched the scar on his cheek.

Rummmmbbbllleeee. . . . The walls around them shook, and the floor heaved. The two old men staggered to keep their balance.

Mori reached out toward Koga. "Come with us, old friend,"

Koga turned back to look at all that gold.

223

"Please," Mori beseeched him. "For the sake of those two little boys!"

"Yes," Koga muttered and started to run, following Mori and the kids up the dark stairs and back into the shrine room.

Ruummmmbbbllllleeee . . .

The shrine room was shaking, too.

"Oh, no!" Rocky suddenly remembered. "The stone entranceway is closed!"

"Where's the sword?" Mori shouted.

"There!" Rocky ran to the table, yanked the sword out, and slid it into the slot in the stone wall.

"Where's the dagger?" Mori shouted.

"Oh, uh, I've got it," Tum Tum said. He started to go through his bag. "It's in here somewhere."

RUUMMMMBBLLLLEEEEE . . . The floor was starting to buckle. Everyone had to dodge the bricks and stones that were falling out of the ceiling.

"Hurry!" Rocky shouted at him.

"We're gonna get crushed!" yelled Colt.

"Find it," Mori urged him.

Tum Tum searched through the bag, tossing out Hershey wrappers, orange peels, and pieces of broken Oreo cookies.

He pulled out a brown-and-white package.

"Hey, I finally found my Ding Dongs!" he cried.

"Get a grip!" Colt shouted at him. "Find it!"

"I'm looking! I'm looking!" Tum Tum cried.

"Remember!" Mori gasped. "The more you want something the harder it is to achieve."

"Uh, right." Tum Tum squeezed his eyes closed and dug around in the bag, chanting, "I *don't* want to find it. I *don't* want to find it!"

"Well?" Rocky yelled.

"Oh, yeah, now I remember." Tum Tum opened the secret compartment under the bag. He took out the dagger and stuck it in the slot in the wall.

Creeaaakkkk! The stone wall shuddered and opened slowly. Mori, Colt, Miyo, and Tum Tum ran through. As Rocky followed, he pulled the dagger out of the stone. Koga came last and pulled out the sword.

The door started to swing closed behind Koga. He looked down at the sword in his hand, knowing that with it he could come back someday and reclaim that enormous treasure if he wanted.

But that was no longer what he really wanted. Just before the stone door slammed shut, Koga threw the sword back inside it.

Thunk! The stone door shut. The sword lay inside. The cave of gold was locked forever.

RUUUUUMMMMMBBBLLLEEEE . . . The entire underground system of passageways was heaving and shaking, threatening to collapse and crush everyone. They all ran, but Tum Tum fell tripped.

Crack! Suddenly his foot fell through the rotted step of an ancient wooden staircase. Tum Tum desperately grabbed his leg and tried to pull his foot out. It was no use! He was stuck!

Koga ran past him and then stopped. Pieces of stone were falling out of the ceiling. The air was filled with dust. Koga knew if he kept going he'd be safe. If he went back and helped that little kid, they might both be crushed.

Koga looked ahead. Safety was only a few dozen yards away. He took another step, then stopped and looked back at Tum Tum. The boy stared back at him with wide pleading eyes, knowing this bad man was his only hope.

Koga no longer wanted to be a bad man. He ran back, grabbed Tum Tum, and yanked him free. Together they raced down the passageways, reached the wall ladder, and climbed up and out into the warm Japanese night.

They'd made it! Everyone fell to the ground, gasping for breath and glad to be alive.

"Oh, man, that was close!" Colt said with a sigh.

"Yeah, I can't believe we made it!" Rocky cried.

Suddenly the rumbling stopped. Everyone braced themselves for a loud crash as the system of underground passageways collapsed, but it didn't come. Mori smiled to himself. He knew Koga's men were still down there. Now they wouldn't be crushed.

Suddenly there was a shout. The kids and Mori looked up and found themselves surrounded by several of Koga's men, aiming guns at them. Koga rose to his feet.

Mori and the kids tensed. Had it all been a trick?

Koga barked something in Japanese at the men, and they lowered their weapons and turned away. The man in black turned to Mori.

"A true ninja is free of all desire," Koga said solemnly. "It has taken me a long time to understand this, Mori Shintaro. From our days as boys in Konang until this moment."

Mori nodded and turned to the kids. "I always said he was a slow learner."

Nearby, one of Koga's men held open the door of his limo. Koga walked past him, got into the black van, and drove away by himself.

The kids gathered around Mori, who smiled proudly at them. "You were brave ninjas, all of you."

Rocky saw that his grandfather's eyes had stopped on Miyo.

"Grandpa," he said. "This is Miyo, the champion of the Konang *dojo*."

"You?" Mori's eyebrows rose in surprise, but then he caught himself and smiled. "A young lady?"

Miyo nodded. Rocky handed the dagger to his grandfather.

"Then I came to give this dagger to you," Mori said. He gestured for Miyo to kneel before him and bow her head.

"As this was presented to me by a ninja master," Mori said, "I pass on the dagger to you, who has achieved the highest ninja level. Mastery of mind . . ."

"Body," added Tum Tum.

"Spirit," added Colt.

"And heart," added Rocky, giving Miyo a meaningful look.

Mori held out the dagger. Miyo lifted her eyes and accepted it reverently.

"Keep this dagger until the day that you, too, will present it to a young master," Mori said.

Miyo bowed and rose, turning to the boys. "This is better than winning the World Series."

"Too bad we missed our game," Colt said with a shrug. "But this was worth it."

"I thought your game wasn't until Sunday," Miyo said.

"Today's Friday," Colt said. "It's still morning back home."

"Hey, if we can get a flight tonight . . ." Rocky said.

"One day to get back," Mori said. "You could make it!"

"*Scramble!*" Tum Tum shouted.

Chapter 17

The game was due to begin in a few minutes. Sam Douglas stood in the front hall of his house, looking at a photo of his boys in baseball uniforms. Jessica stepped into the hall and saw him.

"Kind of quiet around here without the team, huh, Coach?" she asked.

Sam nodded sadly. "They don't even seem to care what I think anymore. They listen more to their grandpa than to me."

"Maybe they listen to Mori because he listens to them," his wife replied softly.

"I just don't understand why they can't be more like . . ." Sam's words trailed off.

"More like you?" Jessica asked. "Because they're not you. They're Samuel and Michael and Jeffrey."

Sam nodded and looked down at the photo again. "Rocky, Colt, and Tum Tum."

Jessica stared at him, surprised. "That's the first time you've ever used their ninja names."

"Yeah, well, when you can't beat 'em, I guess you have to join 'em," Sam replied.

"Talking about beating them, what are you going to do about the game?" Jessica asked.

Sam shook his head slowly. "Guess I have to go over to the field and tell them we can't play."

They drove over to the ballfield. As Sam got out of the car, he saw that the Mustangs were in their dugout, eager to go. In the Dragons dugout, six boys watched him with hopeful eyes. Sam couldn't bear to look at them. He walked over to the announcer's table, where the home plate umpire was standing, talking.

"You the coach of the Dragons?" the ump asked.

"Yes," Sam replied.

"Your team ready to play?"

"Six of them are."

The ump frowned. "You can't play with only six players."

"What are you gonna do, Coach?" the announcer asked.

"I guess I have no choice," Sam said with a shrug. "We have to forfeit."

The announcer and the ump exchanged a look. Then the announcer flicked on his microphone. "Ladies and gentlemen, I'm sorry to have to relay this to you, but because of a shortage of players, the Dragons have announced — "

"*Play ball!*" the shout came from the parking lot, where the boys, Miyo, and Mori jumped out of a cab and raced toward the field.

A grin broke out on Sam's face.

"Okay," shouted the ump. "You heard 'em! Play ball!"

The boys ran into their dugout and quickly introduced Miyo to their father and the other players. Miyo already had her Dragons uniform on. She tucked her hair up under her baseball cap and sat down on the bench.

The game began with the Dragons in the field. The first Mustangs batter was the kid named Darren. Rocky pitched. Darren hit a grounder to third, but the third baseman bobbled the ball and he was safe at first.

As the next Mustangs batter stepped toward the batter's box, the announcer recollected the previous week's game. "The big question on everyone's mind today — will this be a baseball game, or just another wrestling match?"

The Mustangs batter stepped to the plate. Darren started to take a big lead off first. At shortstop, Colt was keenly aware that the Mustangs player might try to steal second base.

Behind the plate, Tum Tum gave Rocky a sign. Rocky leaned back and delivered.

Whiff! As the batter swung and missed, Darren broke for second. Tum Tum jumped up and heaved the ball to Colt, who'd moved over to make the tag.

Once again Darren overshot the bag with his spikes out, trying to nail Colt, who deftly made the tag.

Colt knew Darren had tried to spike him. Anger flashed through his eyes for an instant and he jutted out his fist as if to strike. But then he opened his hand and helped Darren to his feet. The Mustangs player scowled at him, and Colt smiled.

"These Dragons look like a different team than the one we saw last week," the announcer was saying. "They're working together like a well-oiled machine."

The game stayed close. The Dragons were prepared for everything the Mustangs could dish out. When a runner for third tried to knock Tum Tum over and score, Tum Tum bounced the kid back with a sumo stomach thrust.

Going into the top of the sixth inning, the Mustangs were ahead by two. With two outs, the Dragons had Tum Tum on third and Rocky on second. Colt stepped up to the plate.

"With two men on, a base hit might tie this game up," shouted the announcer. "And here's the pitch!"

Whiff! Colt took a big swing and missed completely.

"Strike one!" yelled the home plate ump.

"Hey, swings like a rusty gate!" shouted the Mustangs third baseman.

"Yeah, no stick, batter, no stick!" yelled the shortstop.

Colt felt rattled, but he knew he had to try and settle down.

"Lay off the high ones!" Tum Tum yelled.

Colt rolled his eyes. Everyone was giving him advice. He got ready for the next pitch.

"Careful, Colt," said Gerald, the Mustangs catcher. "Pitcher's a little wild today."

The Mustangs pitcher delivered a brushback pitch high and inside. Even as Colt lurched backward to avoid being hit, he swung.

Whiff!

"Strike two!" yelled the ump.

"Hey, Colt," Gerald, the Mustangs catcher said with a laugh. "I thought you just threw like a girl. I didn't know you hit like one, too!"

Meanwhile, Rocky took a lead second. "Only the good ones, Colt," he yelled.

Colt stepped out of the box and spit into his batting gloves. "Try one over the plate!" he yelled at Darren, the Mustangs pitcher.

"You won't hit it anyway," smirked Gerald.

Colt stepped back up to the plate and dug his cleats in. Darren rocked and delivered. Colt started to swing. Suddenly he realized it was a change-up! He was too far out in front of the ball. He tried to hold up, but it was too late.

Whiff!

"Strike three!" yelled the ump.

"The same pitcher who got you on last game!" Gerald shouted gleefully at Colt. "Man, you don't learn!"

"Dude can't even hit the easy ones," muttered Darren as he passed Colt on his way to the dugout.

Colt felt his face burn. It felt as if steam were hissing out of his ears. He threw his bat and helmet to the ground and kicked a spray of dirt.

"Aw, look, he's mad!" yelled the Mustangs second baseman as he jogged past him. The other Mustangs laughed.

Sam yelled at him from the dugout. "You lose your temper one more time and I'm going to take you out of the game!"

Colt hung his head, got his mitt, and headed for shortstop.

By the bottom of the ninth, the Dragons were trailing three to four. Sam put Miyo in center field after the regular center fielder got hurt. With two outs and the bases loaded, Keith came up to bat. Rocky knew that if Keith got a hit, it would probably put the game out of reach for the Dragons. He took a deep breath, rocked, and delivered.

CRACK! Just from the sound of the bat, Rocky knew it was hit solidly and was probably gone. He spun around on the pitcher's mound and watched Miyo streaking back toward the fence.

There's no way she can get it, Rocky thought sadly. No way!

But Miyo kept streaking back.

Closer.

And closer . . .

At the very last moment, Miyo dove, glove outstretched, as the ball hurtled down over her shoulder.

Plap! The ball hit her mitt and stayed in the webbing.

"She caught it!" Colt screamed. He and the other players raced into the outfield where Miyo stood proudly, holding the ball aloft, and surrounded her.

They all headed for the dugout together.

"Okay, team." Sam clapped his hands together. "This is it. Our last chance. One run ties the game. Two runs means we win. Let's get out there and do our best."

The kids took their seats on the bench. Sam gestured to his sons and stood in the corner talking quietly to them.

"Listen, boys," he said quietly. "I just want you to know that, win or lose, I'm proud of you. You're acting like real sportsmen out there. I told you, you learn about life through baseball."

The boys glanced at each other.

"Uh, with a little ninja thrown in," Sam added. "Anyway, I'm glad to have you home, men."

The boys each pulled a baseball bat out of the bat supply and pushed the bat heads together.

"Four strands of rope," Colt said.

Sam put his hand in. "Four strands of rope."

The boys grinned. "Now let's murderlize them," Tum Tum cried.

The first Dragons batter struck out. The

second hit a grounder back to Darren on the pitcher's mound and was thrown out at first. With two outs, Tum Tum came to the plate. The Mustangs pitcher started his motion. Tum Tum squared to bunt, but as the infielders rushed in, he quickly jumped back and swung, blooping the ball over the third baseman's head.

Rocky was up next. *Crack!* He nailed a line drive into shallow left and ran to first. Tum Tum ran to second.

Colt got up to the plate.

"Hee-haw!" Darren called.

Colt just smiled. Darren glared at him and threw.

Whiff! Colt took a mighty cut and missed.

"Strike one!"

"Here we go again!" laughed Gerald behind the plate.

Colt felt as if he was going to explode, but he forced a smile on his face. At first and second base, Rocky and Tum Tum looked gloomy. They knew what always happened when Colt got behind in the count.

Darren threw again.

Whiff!

"Strike two!" yelled the ump.

In the Dragons dugout, the players groaned and stared down at the floor. Sam Douglas shook his head sadly.

"Two strikes, two outs," shouted the announcer. "One more strike and the Mustangs win the championship."

Colt stood ready to swing, but at the last second, he raised his hand. "Time, ump." He backed out of the box and took a deep breath. Everything rested on this next pitch. *Everything!* Colt glanced over at the stands where Grandpa Mori sat with his mom. Mori gave him a nod of encouragement.

He stepped back into the batter's box. This time he'd wait on the pitcher. He'd see what he had.

Darren threw. Colt swung.

Crack! It felt good, really good! The ball sailed up in the air down the left field line. It was gone! Colt was sure of it. It just had to stay fair.

"*Yah-hoo!*" Tum Tum and Rocky jumped up and down cheering as they started to round the bases.

"Come on! Come on!" Colt skipped down the first base line, watching the ball and waving it fair.

At the very last second, the ball hooked into foul territory.

"Foul ball!" the ump shouted.

Rocky and Tum Tum staggered to a stop, their mouths agape in bewilderment. Colt stumbled to his knees in disappointment. The anguished silence of the moment was broken by laughter coming from the Mustangs.

Colt trudged back to home plate.

"Just a long foul ball," Gerald said with a smirk. "No way you're gonna hit that ball twice, chump."

Colt picked his bat up from the ground and realized it had cracked. He'd have to get a new one. He jogged back to the dugout, aware that every Dragons player had pinned his hopeful eyes on him. Miyo handed him a new bat.

"Strength in control," she whispered.

Colt nodded and walked back to the plate. He could hear his grandfather's words, *"Focus. Wait until it gets as big as a bull's-eye . . ."*

Colt stepped up to the plate and

squeezed the bat's throat. The pitcher delivered. Colt focused until he had tunnel vision. The ball grew bigger and seemed to slow down. Colt swung.

CRACK!

Colt dropped his bat and didn't move. Gerald straightened up and flicked off his mask. They stood side-by-side watching as the ball sailed toward the centerfield fence.

"It's back!" the announcer shouted. "Back . . . back . . ."

Crash! The ball smashed through the scoreboard.

The crowd started to roar. Colt turned to Gerald and smiled. "See you around, *chump*," he said, and started around the bases on his victory run.

"Holy cow!" the announcer shouted. "What a shot! That's it! The Dragons win the game six to four. They're our new league champions!"

Colt was so happy he did ninja handsprings all the way from third base to home plate! The team crowded around him, cheering. In the stands, Jessica hugged Mori. On the field, Sam hugged all his players.

Soon the celebration calmed down, and

the players headed for the parking lot. Rocky and Miyo held hands as they walked.

"You'll show them when you get back to Konang, that's for sure," Rocky said.

"Yes," replied Miyo.

Ahead, Colt spotted Keith, Darren, and Gerald from the Mustangs waiting for them.

"Uh-oh," he said in a low voice. "I think they want the game to go into extra innings in the parking lot."

As the three ninjas got to the parking lot, the Mustangs players stepped into their paths.

"You guys won the first round, huh?" Keith snarled.

"But the game ain't over yet," said Darren as he smacked his fist into his hand.

Keith and Darren gave Colt a shove.

"Colt," Rocky cautioned, stepping between them.

"I can handle this." Colt waved his brother away and faced Keith. "Tell you what, tough guy. We'll go one on one. You choose your best guy to fight any one of us."

Keith nodded at the other Mustangs and

stepped forward. Miyo started to back away from the group.

"Hey, wait a minute," Keith said to her. "I pick you. You ruined my home run, girl."

Tum Tum stood in front of Miyo. "Oh, come on. She's just a girl."

"Hey, she played on a guys' team," Keith argued. "That means she plays by guys' rules."

"But she's just visiting," Tum Tum said. "Pick me instead. I'll fight you."

But Keith stepped toward Miyo. "Come here," he growled.

Miyo looked down shyly as the three ninjas backed away, trying not to let their smiles be too obvious.

Tum Tum winked at Rocky. "Well, I tried."

Rocky nodded. "Guess the guy wants to play by guys' rules."

"*Eeeeeiiiii-yahhhh!*" Miyo let out a bloodcurdling scream and jumped in the air, ready to kick Keith's head in.

"*Ahhhhhhh!*" With a collective scream of terror, the three Mustangs players turned and ran, leaving a cloud of dust. The three ninjas and Miyo shared a high-five.

"We won the world series!" Miyo cried with joy.

The three ninjas glanced at each other and smiled.

"We sure did," Tum Tum replied, and they all laughed.